T0375711

RENEWAL

RENEWAL

WRITTEN BY
MICHELE GORZNEY

authorHOUSE®

AuthorHouse™
1663 Liberty Drive
Bloomington, IN 47403
www.authorhouse.com
Phone: 1-800-839-8640

Published by AuthorHouse   10/12/2012

ISBN: 978-1-4567-9900-7 (sc)
ISBN: 978-1-4567-9899-4 (ebk)

I dedicate this book to my daughter and her friend, for without our little adventure this book would have never been written. I love you McKinzey!

Prologue

How would one begin to tell of the beginning of such true evil? Who would even want to bring these creatures to the world? Evil, pure and true Evil! The kind of evil that has no end and no beginning so, why would this evil bring these creatures to life? Because it could! Because it wanted to tip the scales from good to evil, giving them each a power that only they could control. To give you a short version of what these evil creatures are, simple put, they are vampyers. There are twelve of them, six males and six females. All of them wanting and needing nothing more than to do Evils work. However, Good is always around to fight the good fight, even if it means death!

They are where it all started. They alone could make more vampyers. They were very meticulous about who they would turn. The human had to have evil within them for the Twelve to choose them. However, as time went on they had chosen hundreds of thousands of these lesser vampyers. The ones that they made did not have any special powers of their own. Only to kill and feed from the humans.

As in every good and evil there is the good that tries to stop the evil. Vampyer killers could kill the lesser vampyers but could not kill the Twelve. Not even a lesser vampyer could do that. No one knew how or what would kill them. They tried the stake in the heart and even tried cutting off their heads. But to get too just one of them was impossible. They were one. They felt, breathed, needed as one. If one felt as if they were going to be harmed the other eleven were there in a blink of an eye.

Now comes the current day. The Year is 2009. The Twelve have made themselves very comfortable and have no worries of being taking out. The humans of this time feel comfort in the tales of vampyers. They no longer fear them or hunt them as they once did.

Chapter One
The Blood

"Hey Mom let's go in Hot Topic please. I want to see what new vampyer stuff they got in." Crysta, my daughter, begs me.

"Oh sure I just love coming in here." I tell them.

"Crysta look at these cool gloves." Leeha, my daughter's best friend, hands them to Crysta. Leeha has been like a second daughter to me and has always called me Mom.

"Ok I am going to look around a bit see if there is anything that I might like." I tell them.

That is how it all started. I am Mikatta Hope. I am a widow and a Mother of two kids in their twenties. I am five feet and four inches tall with blonde hair and blue eyes. My daughter Crysta is twenty-two, and a carbon copy of me except, she is five feet and seven inches. She loves being just that little taller than me. My son Grady is twenty-five and looks just like his dad did with blonde hair and blue eyes. He is almost six feet tall. We live in Colorado Springs where we have lived since my late husband and I moved here over twenty-one years ago. I like living here with the mountains so close to the city. It makes having nature and the comforts of a mall all with in driving reach. I had no idea of what was to become of my little family and still can't believe what has happened to us. Even so, I am getting ahead of myself . . .

"Hey girls, you have got to see this!"
"What is it Mom?" Crysta asks.

"You know how you ALWAYS say I am a vampyer? Well, they have this packet that looks like blood. It's an energy drink!"

"Wow that is wicked cool Mom you should get it." Leeha laughs. Leeha is Crysta's best friend. Her family used to live right next door. About a year ago they moved about an hour away from us. So the girls don't get to see much of each other these days.

"That is so you Mom, it really looks like real blood."

"Well you know me. I so have to try it" I laugh as I grab the blood packet and take it to pay for it. We shopped some more before we left the mall. As I was driving us home I tell the girls . . .

"Ok I have to taste it right now it is driving me nuts!"

As I open it up and drink I get a very funny feeling that seems to run throughout my whole body. Like my body is screaming for more, more of this wonderful drink.

"Wow that is really amazing! And I can tell already that it has a wicked kick to it."

"Let me taste it Mom?" Leeha asks.

"Ok here just don't drink it all please, I really like it!"

"You're right it is really good!"

"Crysta would you like to taste it?"

"Oh fine give it here, even though it looks gross!" Crysta is not one with a tough stomach. Even so, she was still really into the vampyer stuff as well so she just had to try it.

"Well I am not loving it but it does have something."

"I think I am going to have to buy more of that stuff. I already want to drink more." I did I really wanted more.

As luck would have it we had two stores that were selling the little blood drink. After I had drunk the first one I felt aware. More awake than I had since I lost my husband. This was the most alive I had felt in over two years. So I really wanted more. The girls thought I was just being a goof, but they were all for me being in a better mood than I had been in, so they went and purchased a ton of the drink for me. Leeha liked the drink as well, and Crysta, well let's just say that she enjoyed the feeling that it gave her but was not wanting to drink anymore of it due to the real blood likeness it had. After about a week of having like two or three of these a day I started to noticed a change . . . a change in me!

"Hey I heard that Grady! Stop talking to your sister like that and remember you are not her father." Grady comes running up the stairs from his room two floors down from me with a look on his face. I can't even describe.

"How in the hell did you hear that?" Grady asks me with a touch of fear in his voice.

"Does it really matter? You can't tell her who she can date young man you are not her parent!"

"Really Mom how did you hear that? I wasn't yelling or even talking loud to her. I was just telling her what I thought?"

"I have vampyer ears you pain remember I can hear everything! Now stop telling her who she can date, understand?" With a very unusual look on his face he tells me . . .

"Yea . . . Sure . . . whatever you say Mom."

I don't think I can say I have ever seen him look at me like that before. He would have rather stood there and fought with me about it for as long as he thought he could get away with fighting with me. But his face is what really got me. How could I have heard him? I mean really they were all the way down in his room, which is two floors beneath me. That was the first thing that started to show signs of something in me changing. I didn't want to tell the kids, I wasn't sure that it was anything for them to worry about. They have worried about me so much lately. In fact, they came back just because they felt that I needed them with me, after their Dad passed away. I fell into a very dark place, and I didn't want to come back from it. Losing my husband had really changed me. I married Kevin and I believed that I would never be apart from him. Now I am going through yet another change in my life, and again, I have to go through it without him. I just want to go outside, sit on our swing and look at the moon. That has always calmed me, living in the city you can't really see the stars that well. So I liked looking at the moon.

Chapter Two
The Makers

"I am tired of the old ones telling us what we can and cannot do!" Nathan paces back and forth, trying to keep his temper under control.

"What would you have us do Brother? They are our makers and you know there is nothing that we can do. We can't make our own followers. Only the Old ones can make new vampyers."

"You're a genetics doctor you can't tell me that you have no idea how we could make our own vampyers?"

"I have been thinking about something . . . but am not sure if it is even something that can work." Justin ponders something that he has thought about ever since he became a vampyer.

"Well we will never know unless we try it!" Nathan has wanted to have his own followers for over one hundred years now. He has tried to make his own vampyers but only the original twelve can make new ones.

"Ok but you will have to bleed a lot for me! And I do mean a lot!"

Justin's plan was to mix their blood with a drink so that humans would drink it. When their blood was consumed enough by a human with the right mix of chemicals it should bring on the change. They knew it wouldn't work on all humans. The human genetic makeup is different in every human. So it wouldn't work on all humans. But they wanted to find out what humans it would work on. If it would work at all!

"Nathan I think I have found a human that our blood might be changing!"

"Are you sure? You know how many times you have said this and nothing is really changing in them?"

"I am sure! And she can't seem to get enough of the drink. She drinks at least four packets a day!" Justin says with so much hunger in his voice that Nathan has to calm him.

"Now, now my brother calm down we will send her a case of the drink and see if we can hurry the change along."

"I think we should be careful with that. Let the change come along at a normal rate! We don't know what things are changing in her. We should just be careful."

"Send her the case NOW Justin!"

"Ok I will send her the case, but I will watch her closely so I can see how she is changing. I need to know what is changing in her and if it will turn her all the way or not!" Justin says as he thinks of the possibility of her being one of them soon, doing what they wanted her to do.

"Do what you must brother but I want her to be ours soon. We will need to test her blood so we can find what part of her allows the change to happen. I want our own vampyers and I want them NOW!"

"Brother we don't know everything about her yet! We need more time to understand her and why the blood is affecting her."

Justin was very afraid that with her being the only one that was changing this fast from their blood, that maybe she might become something different from them and that would not be good. What if they were making something

that wasn't vampyer or human. What if she was becoming
something else? He had been running some tests, and found
that some genes would split and only one of the strands
would be the stronger. But the second strand didn't go
away just didn't change. If this second strand changed as
well what would that make this person? Not human yet not
vampyer!

Justin tried to tell his brother this but Nathan didn't care
he wanted his own slave vampyers. She was changing and
that is all that Nathan cared about. So they sent Mikatta a
case full of the blood packets.

"Oh my God! Crysta you have to come see this!"

"What on earth are you getting so worked up about
Mom?"

"Look the makers of the blood energy drink that I like
sent me an entire case of the stuff with a letter that reads . . .
Dear Mikatta, thank you for purchasing our new energy
drink. We would like to say thank you by sending you this
case of Blood Energy packets. You could call it a buy one
get one free. Again thank you for purchasing our product."

"Great now you have a large supply of your favorite
drink! You know I think that stuff has changed you Mom!"

"Your right I think it has given me that pick me up that
I have needed."

"It is changing you in other ways too. Like you don't
sleep very much anymore, you have lost a lot of weight and
I believe that your eyes are changing color!"

"Well I don't see those things as bad things. I think that it is good that I have lost some weight. My hair is even growing longer than I have been able to get it in a long time. So stop worrying! I am fine and I wouldn't do anything that would hurt myself you know that."

"I know I just worry about you Mom I love you and don't want anything to happen to you!"

I have noticed other changes in myself but haven't told my kids of these things because even I didn't understand them. My eyes had changed color. They had turned almost violet. I felt really strong. Not just a little stronger but like I could lift a car if I wanted to. Yet I haven't tried it out. The weight loss was another thing I wasn't really sure of. Five maybe ten pounds I could see but thirty in less than a month? I could hear extremely well like I could hear someone that was four houses away from me. Yeah that is so not normal. But I liked the way I was feeling. I felt young, strong and in control for the first time in years! I could smell things that I had never smelled before as well. Some things were really wonderful. Then there was a smell that seemed bad, yet I was drawn to it. I wanted it. Night would come and I would feel more energy than I did feel during the day. I couldn't sleep at all, not during the day, not during the night. I could see even better. I wore contacts for more than half my life. I hadn't had to put them in for weeks. The worst part is that I really craved the blood energy drinks. I needed them. Like nothing else I have ever craved. I needed them. If I didn't drink at least one a day my body would ache. I wanted the drink and always had it with me.

The days go by so fast now that I don't sleep. I think that there isn't one wall, drawer or room in my house that isn't spotless.

I can't sleep, not at all, so I move and I think about things that are very strange. As I move my thoughts wander from things like how strong I have gotten and what if I was a superhero! Funny thinking about how maybe you could move so fast to save a child from being hit by a car or you could lift something very heavy off of a person and get them to safety. I really was dreaming I think. I mean really how could any of that even be real? Then I would have thoughts of drinking real blood. I would crave it. I worried that I was just having sleep deprivation, and everything was just starting to run together. Then there was my son's face. I couldn't get it out of my mind. He had even done everything he could so that he could avoid me. That was nothing like him, we have always had a wonderful relationship. He looked scared! Scared of his own mother? How could that even be possible? I had to talk to him it couldn't wait this needed to be fixed right now.

"Grady wake up I really need to talk to you!"

"God Mom it is two in the morning. Can't this wait until I was you know really awake?"

"NO it can't I can't stop thinking about it, and I need to know why you looked at me the way you did the other day when I told you not to tell your sister who to date?"

"Really Mom it was nothing."

"Grady Scott Hope I gave birth to you and have watched you your whole life. Do not sit there and LIE to me now!"

"Ok, ok you really want to know?"

"I would not be in here at two in the morning if I didn't!"

"When you were talking to me your eyes changed. And I am not talking in just color, because they seem to do that a lot lately. But they changed shape somehow, almost tiger like or something."

"You must have just imagined it you know that is impossible. Really maybe I was squinting?"

"Mom I know what I saw. They turned deep purple then changed to the shape of a tiger or something like that. I can't be sure because I don't believe I have ever seen anything like it."

"I . . . that . . . . you must . . . That just can't be?"

"I have wanted to tell you for a while now that you are changing in more ways then what most people can see. You are more aware then I can even imagine. Your hearing is like nothing any human would ever dream of having. You are much stronger than even me and don't you dare say all of this is not true. Because I have been watching you these past few days and I have seen you do some things that are just not possible."

"And what do you think I am becoming?"

"I think it has to do with those energy packets that you have been drinking. I noticed the changes beginning right after you started drinking them. I think you should find out where they come from and who is making them and what exactly they are putting in them!"

"Well they just sent me another case of them. There is a return address on the box I could start there."

"I am going with you. I don't want you going after whatever this could be alone."

"Grady, have you been drinking the packets?"

"Ha why would you even think that? No Mom, no way!" At that moment my son couldn't look me in the eyes and I knew he was lying. He could never look me in the eyes and lie. He just couldn't do it.

"You're lying to me and you know it! You have been drinking them. Have you been feeling things change in yourself as well?"

Grady hangs his head and still not looking me in the eyes tells me . . .

"Yes. I have been. When I noticed how it was making you feel so much stronger and younger I thought it couldn't hurt. With all the sports that I am trying to keep up with I figured that I could use the extra boost."

"Then you noticed the other changes that the drink brings as well, like the hearing and the vision. Why didn't you say something to me?"

"Because, Mom, I didn't want you to be mad at me for drinking your energy packets."

"For the love of it all you should know better than that. I would have only been mad for a day or two." Grady and I laugh. That is the first time we have been comfortable with each other in weeks.

Ok so now here we are my son and I trying to track down whomever it is making these wonderful little packets of blood for us to drink. I see in my son's eyes the change in color that I have noticed in my own. I also notice that he has gotten a little buffer in the arms and chest and leaned out quite a bit. He walks with a confidence that he hasn't ever had before. I am proud, for some reason, yet scared. It was one thing for me to be going through this strange change, but to have my son going through the same thing at the same time? I am worried for him and I do not want anything to harm him. I start to feel something build inside me, every part of my being is tensing up and I have the need to hurt something. Calm, calm I tell myself, you do not want to hurt any of these people. You know that you could kill them with all of this power you have. You're not mad at them. It is these things or whatever they are that have changed you. That is where you need to focus your anger.

"I don't think that this is the right place Mom. It doesn't look like anyone has used this place for years."

"Well this is the address on the package. Let's just go inside and have a look around. There is no harm in just looking around!"

Inside it looks the same as the outside did. Dust and dirt everywhere, and no signs of anyone being there for many years. We go up the stairs to the second level just to see if there is any sign of anyone ever being there. Again, nothing to show that there has been anyone here for years.

"They must have just used the address so that no one could find them." Grady says with much anger in his voice.

"Did you really think that they would have made it so easy to find them if they even had any idea what this stuff is doing to us?"

"No your right they would not want to be found so easy!"

"I think I might have a way to find them, but we are going to have to continue to drink the packets."

"I had a really sick feeling that you were going to say that. We have no idea what this stuff will do to us if we drink too much of it."

"Well, at this point in time I believe I am too far gone to go back. I am going to see what happens to me when I have consumed enough of this stuff. Let it change me if that is what they want."

"Mom you can't do that what if it makes you . . . . evil?"

"I don't feel evil right now, and I believe that I am very close to whatever change that is going to happen to me. And I believe that when that happens, I will know just where to find whoever it is that is behind this."

"I want to do this with you Mom. I don't want you to go alone. I will continue to drink as well. If you are going to change then so am I."

"You know that is not what I want. I would rather you stay just the way you are son. It pains me to know that you are going through all of this, as well as I am."

"I chose to drink the packets, so I am choosing to stay with you through this whole thing. I will never leave you Mom, not ever."

"Let's go home, I miss Crysta and need to make sure she is doing ok."

The ride home was quite, but I could hear my son's thoughts. It was strange. I felt as if I was intruding into his mind, but I couldn't stop myself. He was worried about me so much. He wanted to be there to protect me form anything and everything that might bring harm to me. Funny, because I was feeling the exact same thing about him. As soon as we pulled into the drive, I could sense something. Not bad just something like me like Grady. And he sensed it as well. We hurried into the house, with speed that was almost scary for us. Inside I followed my feeling, and it leads me right to my daughter.

"Crysta are you ok?"

"Yeah I feel great why?"

"Holy shit Mom she has been drinking them too!"

"Yes son thank you, I had figured that one out before we got in the house. Crysta why have you been drinking the blood packets?"

"Well I told you I noticed changes in you and well with school and all the sports I was getting really tired. I didn't think I could keep up with everything, so I tried a couple. When I started feeling all that energy and stronger I just couldn't stop."

"You have no idea what that stuff is doing to us! It is changing us in ways that I don't believe are normal. Grady and I are trying to find out who sent these to us and what the hell is in them."

"You said that it didn't seem like a bad thing to feel so much better? I was just going off of what you had said."

"I'm sorry I am not mad at you. I just didn't want both of my kids going through this dumb thing. I was fine as long as it was just me. But not my kids you are all I have left and if anything happens to you I would just die."

"I am guessing that with the powers, that we have gained and all the other perks that have seemed to come from this, it will be hard for anything to harm us Mom." Grady stands up and walks over to me and hugs me so tight.

"Together we are stronger. Doing this together is a good thing Mom this way we can take care of each other." Grady's words were strong and firm. I knew that we would all be together for a very long time. Reading their minds I could see that they both were happy about what was happening to us. I wondered if they too could read minds, so I ask.

"Have either of you noticed any other things happening to you?"

"Like what Mom?" Crysta asks

"Anything like . . . well can you read people's minds or maybe move things with your our own mind? I really want to know everything so that we can go in prepared."

"So far just the strength, speed, hearing and wow can I smell things really good now." Crysta laughs.

"Grady?"

"Well, I have all those things as well, but I have noticed that I can jump really, really high. I have jumped to the top of buildings." Grady says with a really proud look on his face.

"Well I can read your minds but not just yours everyone around me. I also have been able to move things by just thinking about it. I get the feeling that there will be more to come when I finish whatever change that is happening"

"Well I want some cool powers!" Crysta pouts. She really hated being the only one that didn't get any special powers yet.

We decided that we were not going to drink the packets fast. Whatever was happening was not hurting us so far so we would continue to drink at the same rate. Until I had drunk my two for the day and my stomach felt as if it was tied up in knots.

"OH GOD!!! THE PAIN, STOP THE PAIN!!" I dropped to the floor, and then my whole body started to shake. My head felt like it was going to explode. The kids where there in an instant.

"Mom here let me hold you so you won't shake so much." Grady pulls me to him, holding on very tight so the shaking would stop. Crysta takes hold of my head, and for some reason I could feel the pressure lesson. I also noticed Crysta's eye's getting bigger, and she was gritting her teeth. I pushed her hands away screaming.

"No. You will have to go through this as well. I don't need you going through it twice. Grady I need blood. I mean real blood not the drink it will stop my shacking."

Grady cuts his arm with his finger nail and puts his arm in front of my mouth. I didn't want to drink it because it was my son, but the smell! I grabbed his arm and began to drink his blood. I loved the sweet metal flavor that was filling me. I pulled his arm away as I felt the shaking slow. I then realized that they would both go through the same thing and would also need to drink blood to stop it. Was it the human part that I tasted? I don't think that was the part of the blood I wanted. The other part of the blood changing part. That is what I was wanting.

"I know what I have become now. I am half human because I still feel my heart beating. But the other half is vampyer. I can sense the blood inside me as two different types of vampyers. I know I can find them by just focusing on them hard enough."

"You're not going to go until we are all changed Mom. You will need us both. If we are only half of what they are they will be stronger than us. It will take all three of us to stop them." Still holding me tight Grady tells me that we will not separate for any reason.

"Ok I think that we are stronger than they are, but it is always better to be prepared for everything."

As I rested from my change, I could feel the need to feed again. However, instead of drinking from my kids I took about ten of the packets and just drank them all. I felt better and knew that it was what I was going to need to live in this new life!

Chapter
Three
The Meeting

In the next few days, both Crysta and Grady, both went through the change as well. I let them drink from me, which seemed to help them almost instantly. My blood was very strong for them. They too craved the vampyer blood. So Now that we were all changed we wanted to find the two vampyers that had changed us. We all focused very hard on the blood within us and before I knew it I could see their faces. Nathan was the first one I was linked to he knew it the minute I was in his head. I could sense the fear he had and I told him . . .

"We are coming for you Nathan. I will drain you of all of your blood for doing this to me and my family!"

"How are you doing this? How can you be in my head so far a distance? How do you know my name?"

I left him to go to the other. Justin was the one who made the packets. He was the one who knew how to do it. Justin was not afraid of me. He spoke to me first.

"I am sorry for the pain that you have had to endure. I did not know that it would do that to you. However, we have made you into what you are so that you can be a better being. I don't know what to call you as of yet, you still have a heartbeat, and that I did not expect."

"Listen to me very carefully Justin! You will not live much longer. My children and I are coming for you and your brother Nathan. I want you dead so you can't do this to anyone else."

"If you kill us so quickly you will not know of all the things you should know about what you are. You might want to take your time and hear me Mikatta. I have watched you from the day you drank your first packet. You were one of the few that started to change. There are others like you and your children. Although I have to say that you three seem to be the strongest of them all. I am proud to call you my daughter."

"I am NOT YOUR DAUGHTER! I am the daughter of Karen and Joseph Murray. They are my parents not a monster like you. No matter what your blood has done to me, you are not my father!"

"Your anger is very strong. I do believe you will come to kill me and my brother. However, you should know that we are not the ones you will have to really worry about. There are twelve that will come for you and they will kill you for being what you are. When they find out what Nathan and I have done they will come for us as well. I want you to kill me daughter. If I am to die, I want it to be you. So I am already coming to you."

"What do you mean twelve? Twelve what?"

"I will tell you before you drink my last drop of blood daughter."

"You better bring your brother. I would hate to have to come after him."

"We are both almost there. We were wrong to change you, and you did not become what we were hoping for. You became much, much more."

There is a knock at our front door. I was there in less than a second. There stood before us Nathan and Justin. I was ready for a fight as was my son. His thoughts were of their blood and how much he wanted it.

"Do I have to invite you in or can you enter on your own?" I asked with all the sarcasm that I could put in my voice.

"An invitation would be polite. But we may enter without one because you are no longer a full human daughter!"

"I am warning you stop calling me that! Tell me about the twelve before I kill you right here and now."

Justin and Nathan walked in and sat down on our couch. Justin was the only one who spoke. He rolled off a story about twelve original vampyers that created them. How the twelve were different from the ones like themselves. Then he decided to tell us why they did what they did with the packets. Telling us how they could only do what their creator wanted them to do. That they have been slaves to the Twelve Original Vampyers for over five hundred years. They thought that by making us, we would be their slaves. Now they would finally be the masters.

"I know now that you are much more than what I had thought you would be. I can feel all the power that each of you hold. I have spoken with Nathan about how you are going to kill all of the vampyers that are out there. And that we will not leave here alive. But I do want to see how powerful you all are, so we are not going down without a fight!"

At that instance, he was on top of me and Nathan had Grady by the throat. Crysta was wicked fast and was behind Justin throwing him off me. I was on Nathan with all my force and before he could even scratch my son my teeth were in his neck and I was drinking his blood. Crysta had turned on Justin and was backing him against the wall as Grady joined her. At the same time they both sank their teeth into Justin's neck and began to feed. I have to say that I was so happy to drink. Nathan tasted so good. Sweet, like honey and yet there was more to it, more that I wanted.

Crysta and Grady were feeling the same as they drank from Justin. I could feel how it made them feel. Then I could feel everything. I was spinning in my head I felt so wonderful. Our bodies began to hum. I could feel both of my children's hearts beat faster and faster in beat with mine. As we drank the very last drop of our maker's blood we stood up and came together in a circle. I held my children as close to me as I could. I needed to have them close to me to help what I was feeling lessen. Crysta was able to take away some of the humming from my body. I could feel everything and I needed to feel much less or my body would ache.

This new-found feeling was something to be awed by. Not only by drinking their blood did the hunger stop, but I found I knew everything they did. So why did he spend the time to tell us what they had done? Grady and Crysta could feel it as well. Justin had said they had been slaves of the twelve for five hundred years but that wasn't totally true. Only Nathan had been alive for that long. Justin was still very new to the vampyer world. Nathan had been the one who wanted to make us. Justin only did it because Nathan wanted to have his own slaves. The twelve were very hard on their children. That is what they called them. Children of the twelve did as they were told and never asked any questions. Oh all the information coming in at once my head was starting to spin and hurt. Crysta drops to the floor, Grady and I kneel down to her trying to catch her before she hits.

"I see them . . . Oh I see them!" Crysta cries almost in sobs. "They are strong they are pure evil! They will know about us very soon, they have one that can read minds, she will learn of us soon. I can't believe what I am seeing right in front of my face. It is like I am seeing them, all of them. Oh God, how are we going to stay alive with all twelve of them as strong as they are?"

"We are more powerful than they are we know this by what has happened here tonight. With all of us together they can't take us." Grady stands up pulling Crysta in his arms. "I am not going to let anything happen to this family."

As I stood up I could feel heat all around me and I begin to glow. The feeling of anyone hurting my kids angered me and I could feel the power inside me grow and build. How could I have this feeling inside me? How does this happen to someone. Happen to me, to my children? What have I done?

Chapter Four
New Power

We now have to learn how to control these new powers that we have gained. Grady has found that he can see things in a different way than Crysta or I. Almost as if he could see through things when he wants, which I was not sure was a good thing for such a young man.

Crysta has very clear visions. It could be of the past it could be of the future. She can call open any past vision that she wants to see. Justin didn't have a lot of time as a vampyer, so she can only call open what his blood gave her. Her voice seems to carry some real command when it comes to getting a normal human to do something that she wants them to do. I have had to remind her that telling a young man that he thinks that she is cute is not what the gift is for.

Me? Well, Nathan had five hundred years in him, and I drained all of it. I know who is maker was Hanzi Fey. He is a wonderful looking vampyer. Not that he needs the good looks to help him along; he has the power of seduction. I thank heavens I did not get that power. What I did get was something I was still not sure of how to control. When I felt angry or even scared I could feel energy build up inside me. Like I was a battery getting a high recharge. And when I hit full it was as if I could focus all the energy wherever I wanted it to go. When it got there, well let's just say whatever was there before was gone. Reading minds was a cinch now I could do it whenever I wanted to, and to whoever I wanted to. Moving things worked the same.

We all could sense the other, what Nathan called lesser vampyers with such ease. We have been tracking some of them down and watching them. I have tried my energy power on a few of them. That power works wonderfully. The other powers such as Crysta's voice are not as powerful on them though. Even so, they have given us a bit of bait for them. She sort of sings and they seem to come to her like moths to the flame.

Grady's new-found vision has helped us in seeing into places where we believe there might be nests. We are not hungry enough yet to drink from any of these lesser vampyers. But we know that the hunger will come again. We know that we will have to drain these Lessers to be full again. And in doing so we have found that we will gain all of the memories and possibly more gifts.

Right now we really need to get a handle on our new gifts that we have just now. My energy gift has saved a few humans from becoming meals. But in doing this, we are exposing ourselves to these Lessers, and that means we are exposing ourselves to the twelve.

I have been having some very unsettling dreams as of the past three nights. And I don't sleep so you should know these are waking dreams. I have dreamed of Nathan's maker. Hanzi, he is so wonderful to gaze at. He comes to me and touches my face. He tells me that he wants me to come to him. His voice is like being held in a warm silk sheet. I don't feel myself pulled to him, but I can't stop watching him and I can't just simply walk away from him. Then he comes at me with his teeth ready for the bite . . . .

"NO! You can't have me!"

"Mom, are you ok?" Grady rushes in to my room.

"I am fine. It was just another one of those stupid dream things. Really, I am fine."

"Do you think that he knows what you are?"

"I don't know. He seems to want me to be a full lesser vampyer. Like he thinks I am just a simple human. I don't think he knows what I am. Hell Grady I don't even know what we are."

"Crysta and I have been thinking about that. We should have some type of name for what we are. We even think that we should come up with it." Grady laughs, something I haven't heard from him in at least a month.

"So have you come up with anything good?" I smile, that Mom, smile that always brings out that little boy in my son.

"Not yet, but that is only because everything that we have thought of sounds sort of evil. We are so not evil so whatever we call ourselves has to sound good"

"Grady, Mom I think I found what we are called. I was looking on the internet and pulled up something on half human half vampyers." Crysta is so excited I think she just might pop. "We are called Dhampirs."

"Well that doesn't sound so bad, sounds a little sexy." I am laughing so hard at this point I think my stomach will begin to hurt.

"That is so wicked Mom that is what we are. Does it give a definition?" Grady is so excited that he can't calm himself down.

"Yea it says that we have all the powers of vampyers and none of their weaknesses. That we have an unusual sense of finding vampyers and killing them."

"Shit, that is so us. Do you think that they have written books about us?" We are all laughing so hard now that we have fallen to the floor.

This is one of our few really and truly happy moments since all this has happened to us. We sit there on the floor just going back and forth about our new-found name. Telling stories of ourselves to each other and laughing more, too bad that these moments are very few.

The hunger has begun to return. Not just for me. Grady and Crysta feel it as well, and we know that we will have to feed very soon. There are a lot of places that have these lesser vamps, and we know that it will be nothing to take anyone of them. Even so, we don't want to draw to much attention to ourselves just yet. There are these three vamps, two guys and a girl, yes I know seems really sick. They have been together for a very long time, and we feel that they will have a good amount of knowledge. Now at this point in time we need to gather as much of it as we can.

"Ok so we have our plan, and we have been over it like a hundred-times Mom, and if I don't eat soon I really think I might just scream. So can we go tonight?" Crysta looks at me with those oh please Mommy please eyes.

"Alright, I do believe that we all could use the food, and we have been over this more than enough times."

"Then I will get Grady, and we can start getting ready. You are still worried that Hanzi is watching you aren't you?"

"Yes I am but I can't worry about that right now." I really couldn't I had to focus all of my energy on what we were about to do. "Go get your brother we should get going."

The building was a two story older apartment building. Nothing special had four flats two on each side. The vamps were on the top level on the right side. Crysta starts to sing her song to the vamps. We know it will not lure them, but it will serve as a distraction. Grady swiftly moves to the front door and up the stairs. Crysta and I leap onto the building and climb to the window. At the same time, Grady, Crysta and I all enter the flat. The three vampyers have found themselves in the middle of the flat wondering what is going on. Grady rushes the three as do I and Crysta. Grady hits them first knocking them to the ground. Crysta's speed has her on top of one of the males still singing to him to keep him confused. I have grabbed the other male and am pinning him up against the wall. Grady with all the ease as picking up a piece of paper has the female in his grasps. We have decided that we were not going to talk to these three but to just eat them. We bite into our victims and began to feed. Again, the rush is intense and wonderful. They try to fight but they really are no match for us three together.

We leave the building within minutes of entering, and feeling very much full. Of both new knowledge and our hunger is once again gone.

Chapter Five
Understanding

"That was way too easy! We need more of a challenge next time. I really want to get a work out killing these things." Grady is such a guy. He just wants to fight.

"I am sure when we meet anyone of the Twelve we will have a real fight on our hands. I myself am very glad that went so well. We got in and out with no noise and no mess." I am trying to remind myself that even I thought they would be a little harder to kill then that.

"Yea and after what I just learned about the twelve I do believe that we should only take them on one at a time. They are true and pure evil. Not that we didn't already know that." Crysta has a very strong attitude about her now. I think her killing that vamp by herself has given her a little confidence. I smile at my two wonderful children. Pride is a very strong feeling when you have it for your children. I can't stop smiling and the kids notice.

"Ok Mom what on earth are you smiling about?" Crysta asks me.

"Nothing just thinking about you two and how proud I am that you have grown up into such wonderful young people. Or should I say Dhampirs." We all laugh at our new-found name.

Again, I find myself in one of those waking dreams of mine. Hanzi is walking right up to me this time arms out stretched.

"I know what you are Mikatta. Please do not be afraid of me. I am drawn to you like I have never been drawn to any human or vampyer in all my life. I need you in a way I have never needed anything or anyone."

"You can't have me! I am not one of you, and I will never let you turn me."

"I don't want to turn you. I need you just the way you are now. The three you killed tonight you only did so to gain more knowledge of us, and because you needed to feed. See I know you to the core of your soul Mikatta."

"Why are you doing this to me, I am made to kill you. That is what I am going to do. You cannot seduce me the way you do your other victims. I am stronger than anything you have even known, and I will kill all of you. One by one if need be."

"Let me come to you alone with no others? Please I want to show you that I have no intention of harming you. I couldn't even if I wanted to. There is a feeling in a part of me that has never felt anything at all. My heart and all it wants, all it needs is to be near you."

"You are trying to trick me. It is what you do. I have seen what you do to get your victims to come to you. How you make them feel that you want them that you need them. I will not fall for it I know you as well Hanzi!"

"You said that I would make them feel that I wanted and needed them. But have I ever told them or made them feel that I loved them?"

I couldn't answer him. Everything that I knew about him was that he did not know what love was. He had no heart he couldn't love anyone. Why would he say that to me?

"You don't love me Hanzi. You are just doing anything that you can to try and get to me. I won't fall for any of your tricks. You don't know what love is, and you don't know how to love anyone."

"Mikatta I have never felt this before, so I can only believe that it is love. I need to see you. Please let us meet. I will not harm you. As you said you are too strong for me to hurt you. What will it hurt for us to meet?"

At that moment, I knew I could kill him, just as he knew I could. It was as if we had some kind of connection. I did want to meet one of the twelve. However, was I truly ready to come face to face with Hanzi?

"You will tell none of your fellow twelve about this meeting, and you will come alone. I will know if you bring anyone else with you, and I will make sure that you don''t live one more day."

"I will NEVER speak of you to them! You are not going to ever be touched by even one of the others this, I swear to you Mikatta. Not one of them will ever touch you. I will have no harm come to you. I can't have it. I told you I believe that I Love you!"

"I will meet you alone. Where would you like to meet me? And I will not have my children anywhere near you as well. My son would tear you to pieces. I do not Love you Hanzi. But I do want to meet you because I need to talk with one of you before we begin taking you out."

"I can only come out at night you know this. And I would be happy to meet you where there are many humans around so that you can keep me in line. Maybe we could meet at a mall perhaps?"

"Fine do you know the one that I live near?"

"Yes of course. Can we meet tonight please?"

"I will be there in an hour. But remember what you have sworn to me to Hanzi."

"I am bound by it."

Now how do I tell my children that I want to go to the mall all by myself? We have not spent any real time away from each other since the change. But I have to go to Hanzi I have to know more about the twelve. If he is telling me the truth about what he believes he feels for me then I need to know. He is made from pure evil, how can evil love good? How could I have this kind of connection to him? I didn't feel anything like love for him, but I could feel him in my heart! What in the hell was that about? I had to know so that meant I had to see him.

"Hey you two, I want to get out of the house for a bit."

"Cool where are we going?"

"No Grady I said I wanted to get out of the house for a little while. I need some time to myself. With everything that has happened and all these feelings I have inside, I need to clear my head. With the two of you here my head is always full." I laugh, so that they are not hurt by my words

"Ok cool just don't be gone to long ok? Or I will have Crysta here look into your future." He laughs too. I know that if I am gone to long that he would have her do it, so I need to make this fast.

"Give me at least a couple hours ok?"

"Ok but that is it, you know we shouldn't be apart. Just in case any of the vamps smell us out, we should all be together."

"I know and you just remember who the parent is here young man."

On the way to the mall I keep going over and over in my head how I would kill Hanzi if he tried anything at all. And wondering what on earth could make evil fall in love with good? The mall is only about ten minutes from our home, but I needed the time to think.

I am standing in the middle of the food court waiting, for the moment, I see him. But before I see him, I can feel him, hear his thoughts as clear, as if he were standing right next to me. He whispers in the air to me.

"Mikatta I feel your heart beating, it draws me to you. I want to be by your side right now, but I will take my time as any human man would. I do not want to use any of my powers against you. Not that they would even work on you my sweet."

"Don't call me that. You do not have my heart. It belongs to me and to me alone!" At the second, I could smell the most amazing scent sweet yet musky. I wanted to drink it so bad my teeth began to show.

"Wait! If that is you that I smell, you better stay away. I don't think that I can control the urge to drink your blood."

"Mikatta the urge is the same for me, but I know that we can control ourselves. You have the gift inside you of control use it on yourself."

"What are you talking about I can't control anything. I can read minds. I can move things, and I can control energy. Those things you already know there is nothing else I have been able to do."

"Mikatta, you are pure good energy. You can control yourself. Just focus on your inner power. I know I am evil and what I can control is anything I want so I am focusing on not wanting to drink from my love."

"It would be easier for me to do so if you would stop calling me your love." I focus on my hunger. I will not bite him. I will not bite him. I will not. And just like that the urge is gone.

"Please sit. I just need to be near you."

"Why did you need to see me Hanzi? You can see into my mind. You already seem to know me. What do you gain by being close to me?"

"My pain has lessened. In what I believe is my heart. From the moment you killed Nathan I have been in pain. Now sitting close to you, I feel much better."

"And why do you think that is? I don't understand how me killing, one of your many children, would connect us?"

"I wish I knew the answer to that. It is also one of the reasons that I wanted to meet with you. Maybe us spending some time together will help us both to understand what we are feeling."

"What we are feeling? You mean what you are feeling! The only thing I feel right now is the strong urge to drain you of all your blood."

"Are you saying you have no other feelings for me? You don't desire me? Want me? You don't need me?" Hanzi has a very strange look on his face. Like one of agitation. Almost as if he was upset that I had no real feelings for him. This stirs something upsetting in me. I know what he wants of me now. I don't love him I have no feelings for him other than to gain all the knowledge that I can by draining him.

"I know that I love you Mikatta! I know that you could love me as well!"

I feel him trying to seduce me through his powers. At first I want to let him have me, let him take me. NO! I am the strong one.

"Hanzi let's go outside. I don't feel comfortable with all of these people here. I don't want them to overhear us. And I don't want any of them to get hurt. Do you understand me?" I try to speak with a sweet tone, a seduction on my own part.

"Yes, I think I would like to let you drink from me. Maybe, if you see what I feel you will know I speak only the truth to you Dear Mikatta." A drink I would be having. But he would not be getting what he wanted from me.

Chapter Six
Dhampirs

As we get outside I began to build my energy up inside me. Slowly, I don't want him to know what I am up to.

"Why do you want me to love you Hanzi? You can have anyone that you want at any time that you want them. Why do you think that you love me?"

"Because you are my true other half, and I desire you in a way I have never felt before. Together you and I can build our own family of vampyers new and stronger than those lesser ones that have no real power."

"You do not truly believe that I would ever create any vampyers at all? I am made to seek you out and to destroy all of your kind. And I could never love you Hanzi. NEVER!"

"Then I believe dear Mikatta that you will have to die. I can't have you running around killing my children now can I? I know you believe that you are strong enough to kill me. But I am pure evil and that is not something that you can kill my dear one."

"Well I am always up for a challenge." I build all the energy at once I make it burn and in a blink of an eye it is knocking him to the ground. He lay there not moving, but I know I have only stunned him.

"Holy shit! I could tell you had some power, but he is one of the twelve how the hell did you do that?" The voice startles me and I look to my right and there stands the most gorgeous blonde haired blue-eyed man I have ever seen. I then remember about Hanzi. We both advance on him. Hanzi is standing like he had never fallen. Now there is a smile on his face.

"I told you dear Mikatta that you cannot kill me. But I must say that did sting a bit."

"I knew that wouldn't kill you. I know now what will. Hanzi dear you said that I could have a drink from you. Are you not going to let me have that now?"

"No dear Mikatta the only one who will be drinking this evening will be me." At that he is on top of me holding me down. I shove him with all my strength and knock him about five feet from me. Then the stranger grabs Hanzi from behind.

"Mikatta I think you should have that drink now!" I needed no more encouragement. I am on top of Hanzi holding his neck to the side with all my strength, and with the gorgeous strangers help, I bite deep into Hanzi's neck. The blood begins to flow with such wonderful tastes. I can't drink fast enough I want it all. Hanzi is struggling but this wonderful stranger is very strong and Hanzi cannot move. I am drinking faster now. My hunger is for his blood and his blood alone.

"No Mikatta, please stop you are killing me." Hanzi says these words in almost a whisper.

"I know dear Hanzi. I told you that I would kill you, and I always keep my word."

I bite back down and this time I drain him of his very last drop of blood. Hanzi's body doesn't just die. He begins to age until there is only bone and then only dust. I draw in a deep breath of air and blow his ashes into the wind. Then I feel the hum. A much stronger feeling this time than I have felt before. I feel my body start to rise off the ground, and I begin to glow. The stranger grabs me, pulls me close to him holding me as tight as he can. I feel him calming my body easing the hum. I also feel him wanting me. This calms me even more for the strangest reason. Because deep inside I want him to want me. I look up into the deep-blue eyes and ask . . .

"What is your name?"

"My name is Dan Edwards. And you are Mikatta the first Dhampir to kill one of the original twelve. I would very much like to kiss you if that would be ok with you?" How could I tell this wonderful man no?

"Yes Dan you may kiss me, but just so you know that I want to kiss you as well so this might take a bit." I give him the sexiest smile I can, and he leans down and slowly starts to kiss me. Then when he knows I can no longer take the teasing, he takes my mouth with more lust than I have ever felt before in my entire life.

I felt them before they even said a word.

"MOM, what in the hell are you doing?" Grady is aggressive and very upset with me and all that I got from his voice not even reading his mind.

"Well at the moment I am being kissed by this wonderful man whose name is Dan thank you very much."

"We can see that. I meant, why did you take on one of the originals without telling us? Is that why you came out by yourself? You wanted to kill him alone without us?"

"STOP IT! No I did not come out her to kill Hanzi all by myself. I came here to gain knowledge of the twelve. Hanzi was trying to seduce me. He believed that he was in love with me. But when I would not return the love, he decided that he was going to have to kill me. Insert Dan here to help me kill Hanzi. Dan please don't take this wrong, but I really could have taken him by myself. But still, I can't thank you enough for coming to my rescue."

"Please it was my pleasure to help you take out one of the twelve. That and getting to kiss you was defiantly a big plus."

"Ok Dan is it? Stay away from my mother, for the moment or I might have to rip your arms off."

"Grady I said to stop it! Look I think we should take this back to the house I don't think me standing out here for everyone to see glowing is something that we should be doing. I need to move fast anyway. It will help with the humming."

Everyone agreed and we ran back to our house. Dan was almost as fast as Crysta. But she made sure to stay ahead of him to prove that she was better. Reading Grady's mind was hurting my heart. He believed that I wanted to kill that vampyer by myself without him to prove I was the strongest of us. How do I tell him I was just trying to get more information? Inside the house I began to calm down, and I sit down on our couch and try to clear my head of everyone. They are all going so fast about everything, and it is starting to hurt my head.

"Ok that is it, everyone stop thinking right now. Crysta I want you to look into Dan's past to see what kind of person he is. That way you can tell your brother here too clam the hell down and stop thinking of ways to hurt Dan."

"Yes Mom I think that would be a really good idea, but Dan, here is like us a Dhampir. So it seems I have to ask for permission to see into his past. His future I can see. So Dan may I please look into your past?" Crysta asks this with her teeth grinding together.

"Yes you may Crysta."

She closes her eyes and stands there for a moment. This can take a few minutes or longer depending on what she is seeing or what she is looking for. But only a few moments go by and then she speaks.

"I am sorry that she left you Dan. I can't imagine not having my family support me through all this. She should have stayed. But I have to say that you have a friend of mine with you. Mom, Leeha is a Dhampir as well!" That part she says in a high pitched squeal that hurts even my ears.

"Yes I have taking in a few others like us. Leeha was the first one I found. I then came across Jordan, Leham and Kara. They all were going through the change. I could sense it and helped them through it."

"Ok this has been one really long night, and I would really like to rest. I know I can't sleep, but I would like to lie down with no one thinking around me so I can try and clear my head a bit. Would that be alright with everyone?" I asked it but not really in an asking way.

"Of course Mikatta you should rest. I should get back to my kids and tell them of this evenings events, and I am sure that Leeha would love to know of Crysta." Dan looks me deep in the eyes with the most amazing care. "May I kiss you good bye?"

"Hey Dan I think you should just go and do your thing for now!"

"Grady Scott! Shut up and go to your room now! You have no right to act this way to Dan. I am an adult, and I will make my own decisions. Do you understand me?"

"Fine but just know Dan that she is my Mother, and I will not let you hurt her." Grady is gone in the blink of an eye to his room.

"To answer your question Dan, yes, you may kiss me good bye." I lean in to him and kiss him with all the passion that I was feeling at that moment.

Crysta takes my hand and walks me to my room. I can't seem to stop my mind all the knowledge I have gained is flooding in like giant crashing waves. I am thinking that maybe I shouldn't have taken all of Hanzi's blood alone I should have had Dan help. The humming is coming back, and I feel the glow start to return.

"Mom you need to have Grady in here with us, so we can help you. Please let us both help you?"

"Ok you can go get him."

The second she leaves, I feel a bolt of electricity shoot right through my body. I scream in pain, and then I see the remaining vampyers of the original twelve standing right in front of me. Grady and Crysta are there in a blink and ask if I am ok?

"Do you see them?" I ask.

"See who Mom? What is going on what do you see?" Grady is holding me tight on the bed, so I won't float up any more than I already have.

"I can see them all eleven of them standing right in front of me. They know what I have done, and they know who I am. Get Dan and the others Crysta. I need as many of us as I can have near me right now I need the energy. Hurry Crysta I don't know how much time I have!"

Crysta is gone in a flash, and Grady is still holding me. I try to draw what energy I can from him and everything around me to keep myself from being pulled to them. It had only been minutes before I could feel Crysta bring all the rest of the Dhampirs to me. They all gathered around the bed. I pulled all that I could from them to keep my energy full. Then I could hear one of the eleven speaking to me.

"I am Belle Burn. And you are Mikatta Hope. You have taken by brother from me, and I do not know how you could possibly do that?" Her tone was firm, and I could feel the power that she held.

"Mom, who the hell is that talking?" Grady is holding me even tighter now. I look around and everyone is looking for what I am seeing and where the voice is coming from. They can hear her as well. I know that is because I have linked myself to all of them to keep me ground here in this place. The eleven are trying to pull me to them.

"You heard her. She is Belle Burn one of the last remaining originals. The eleven are here in some way, and they are trying to pull me to them. You can hear her because I have linked myself to all of you to keep them from pulling me from this place. So Belle, are you scared now that you know that you can be killed?"

"I fear nothing. We are stronger than you all, and you will not get another chance to kill one of us. We know about you now, and we are prepared for you." I can feel the fear in her voice. She is scared and doesn't understand how a half human half vampyer could kill a pure evil vampyer with all the powers that Hanzi had.

"Well if you weren't scared of us, then you wouldn't be here trying to take me from my home and bring me to you, so that you could try your hand at killing me."

"We will not come for you again. I see that you do have power that I do not understand. May I ask you one question?"

"Have at it. I already know everything about you thanks to Hanzi's wonderful tasting blood that has given me more knowledge and even some cool new powers."

"What are you? You have a heart beat yet you will not age, and you have all the powers of a vampyer. Yet you can walk in the day light and not be harmed?"

"Well Belle dear you can call us Dhampirs. But a better definition would be . . . your death!" And with that the eleven were gone.

Chapter Seven
Family

I was able to unlink from everyone now, and felt much better now. Everyone was just standing there staring at me. I could hear all their thoughts, and they were very confused.

"I know you are all wondering what the hell just happened. And you are a little scared that they could get to me like that. But you don't have to be afraid of them. They are very scared that we will be coming for them and are leaving where they are and going to another place that they feel safe at. Belle is their leader so to speak. She was the first one made, by her mate . . . for lack of a better name Satan. As we all know the purest of all evil. However, she could feel that we were made from good. And just so everyone knows. Justin wasn't like the other vampyers. His heart had been good. I know what he did to us was not what we would call good. Nevertheless, Nathan wanted to have slaves Justin wanted to create someone who could kill them. He hated what he had become. So when he used his blood, we got all the good that he had in him. He only used a little of Nathan's blood because of all the power that Nathan had. I mean he was five hundred years old. Justin knew that we would be good because of who we are in our hearts. I thought at first that it was a random thing, that has happened to us. But I know now that our genetics are all about the same. He used something, which bonded his vampyer genes to ours knowing that we would change. He didn't however, know that we would be as powerful as we truly are.

"You said they were scared of us? Does that mean they know about all of us?" Dan asks.

"I am going to have to say yes. I was linked to all of you the whole time. You all gave me one hell of a power boost. They were trying to pull me, or should I say my soul, to them somehow. Not sure how but I could feel all of them. They are just as confused as we are. This isn't something that they have ever been up against. But I have to say, linking me to you was like tying an anchor to myself. They could no longer pull me to them. All of us together was like a strength they had never come up against. So yes they are scared. But don't let your guards down because of that. If they stay together like I think they are going to do we will not be able to kill them. One maybe two at a time, but them all together we wouldn't have a chance."

Dan comes close to me and takes my hand. Grady shoots him a very hateful look. I send a very calming feeling into my son to let him know that Dan is what I want, and that he would never hurt me. Grady looks down in shock, and then his face softens, hugs me and let's go of me. Dan gets on the bed and lies next to me. The rest of our strange family leaves the room. I could hear how they all wanted to talk and get to know each other better.

"Are you ok Mikatta?" Dan's voice is very soft, and I can feel his concern for me in his voice and his heart. I pull him to me and lay my head on his chest.

"I am doing better now that you are close to me. I can't thank you for coming to help me. It wouldn't even be enough. Having you all here truly saved me. They are just so strong." I almost begin to cry. Fear pours through me just thinking of how their power made me feel. As if he could feel what I was feeling Dan pulls me up to his mouth and kisses me soft and caring. Then he holds me and tells me . . .

"I will never leave you, and I will never let any of them harm you! I would die for you Mikatta. I know that we have only known each other for a very short time. But my soul knows yours, and it has to be with you. When I felt you at the mall, my soul knew it had found the other half of it. That is why I found you so easily when you were fighting Hanzi. I know what power you have in you. They cannot kill you Mikatta. They know it, as well as I do."

"How can you know all of this?"

"You were linked to me remember. I have a gift to you know." He laughs as if I would think that he was just a simple Dhampir. "I can sense and feel other's feelings. I also can put an invisible wall or a shield up against these vampyers."

"Now that gift will come in very handy in our future. I know what you mean about your soul. When I looked into your eyes tonight I felt all of me come to life. I could even draw from you energy the second you were with me, helping me kill Hanzi. I know that with you here right now is the only reason I am not still aching and glowing and feeling all of the effects of his blood. You seem to be aiding in my recovery somehow. Even better than when Crysta and Grady are with me."

"Good I am glad I can help ease the hurt for you. There are many things I would love to do for you and to you, but I think we should go make sure that the kids are doing ok. I don't want to over work your wonderful body." Dan's smile is so big, and he is even blushing as he tells me this. I can read the things he wants, and I know I want them to. But he is right tonight is not the time for us. We need to form some sort of plan against the eleven. They know about us now, and they may not be able to kill me, but they can hurt or even kill the others, my kids and Dan's. I will not let this happen.

"I know but can't we just lie here a little longer? I don't think I am ready to be away from you yet. I mean you're still helping to recharge me." I give him my best sweet little-girl face that I can to aid in my need to keep him close to me right now. "Beside you forget I can read all of their minds, and they are just so happy to have found more like themselves that they aren't even thinking about us or the eleven right now."

"Ok, but we should only stay just a bit longer. I want to ask you something, but don't think I am trying to use the way I feel about you as the only reason I am asking this?"

"Ok I would care less your reasons for asking me anything. I am just happy you are here with me."

"Do you think it would be alright if we all moved in together? I think that we all should stay as close as we can. It seems that we have more power when we are all together. It would make it much easier than to have to send Crysta to get us every time you need our help."

"I would love nothing more than to have you here with me whenever I wanted to be close to you. This, by the way will probably be all the time." I send a very warm seductive touch to his chest with my hand, not even sure how I did it, and he pulls me to him again and begins to kiss me very feverishly, even a little rough. Not in a hurtful way in a way that a man who wants a woman would. I can't stop myself from letting him want me, but I can't understand what I have just done to him. I leap from the bed and stand there looking at him in confusion, as he stares back at me with the same look.

"What in the hell was that? I think I just used the touch of seduction on you!" I can feel the terror in my own voice.

"Calm down its ok I don't mind the added boost that it gives what I already want."

"No you don't understand. Hanzi was the vampyer of pure seduction that is how he found and killed his victims. I don't want that power. And I don't ever want to use it on you." I am sobbing at this point. I feel as if I have done something evil something horribly wrong.

"Mikatta my love stop, come here let me hold you please? You are not hurting me, and you are not doing anything that is evil or wrong." I let him take me in his arms, as I am crying on his chest. His warmth and caring begin to fill me, and I start to become calm. "Yes I did feel the extra push when you touched me, but you only did it because you too want to be with me. You just wanted to show me how much you felt for me. Now we know that you can pass that along to me. I think it will be a good thing to have when we have more time to explore each other!" His grin and slow beat of his heart makes me feel so much better.

"Let's go out to the kids I think we need to calm ourselves from this urge." I know that if I don't pull away now that things will be right back where they were moments ago.

"Yea let's go make sure that the family is getting along." Dan takes my hand and leads me into the living room.

"This is so cool Leeha your one of us! I can't even say how wicked that is." Crysta is so happy and excited that her best friend is just like her now. That I think she might pop.

"So kids what do you all think about what has just happened? I know that you could all hear what was going on in there with the eleven. So I need to know what you all think about us having to go up against them."

"Can we at least introduce ourselves first Mom before you go to the let's kill the vamps' thing?" Grady wants so much for me to meet the new Dhampirs.

"Son I know who they are and there is no need for you to introduce them to me. I know their thoughts, as well as I know yours. I am Mikatta Hope, and I know all of you very well right now due to the link that I had with everyone in the room. You can all just call me Mom, and that will make my life a whole lot easier. Besides Leeha is already family, so I feel that you all are our family now. We will need each other for what is to come, right Crysta?"

"Yea from what I have seen we need to stay close and keep very aware of everything that is going on. They won't just lie in wait for us. They will send out there slaves to try and kill us. We really need to all stay together."

"Dan and I agree. We should move the family in together. We are stronger together, and it would save Crysta a lot of running back and forth."

"Yes I would love a break from all the running. Just because I am the fastest doesn't mean that I want to be running back and forth between two homes. They live on the other side of town for the love of it all." Crysta adds.

"I think it would be cool to have more guys in the house. I have been out numbered for years." Grady truly does feel good about them all moving in and that lessens the stress I was feeling about him not wanting Dan to live in the house.

"I think we should start the move as soon as possible. Mikatta is stronger when there are more of us together. And right now I think the eleven want her dead and gone as soon as possible. I can't have anything happen to her. It would kill me." Dan isn't just telling his kids he is telling mine this. Mostly, Grady so he knows that Dan will never leave me for any reason.

"Dan I know you Love my Mother. And even though that is a very strange thing to have happening in such a short time, after everything I have been through in the last four months tells me that anything is possible. So I will give you no more grief over you and her being together."

My mouth almost dropped to the floor. My son saying that it is ok for a man to be anywhere near me, that isn't possible he has never liked any guy that I have dated since his Dad passed away.

"Thank you Grady. Having your approval, even though it isn't needed, is something that I respect. I will never do anything to bring pain to your mother's heart, body or soul. I swear this to you."

"Thanks Dan. I think." Grady shakes Dan's hand then gives him that guy half hug. Yes thank God that is done. I think I was dreading that more than facing the remaining eleven Vampyers.

The move has to happen overnight and fast. Good thing that we can run so fast that it looks like that it was just the wind blowing. The boys are having way too much fun with this. They are racing to see who can get back and forth the fastest with a piece of furniture in their hands. You could not understand how normal this really felt for us. Like all this time, we were meant to be a family. I think that Grady might have a little thing for Kara though. And Leham so thinks that Crysta is the best thing that has ever come his way. He really thinks that she is his soul mate. Crysta can see everything that Leham is thinking for the future, and she does see her with him. For my daughter that is scary. She was almost married, and the wonderful Mr. Right turned out to be a mean and hateful person who thought that my daughter was a punching bag. Grady showed him who was the punching bag and Mr. Wrong left with his tail tucked firmly between his legs. Try to think of yourself being able to see what is going to happen to you in the future. Now see if you could maintain yourself as anything but stressed out. She was trying so hard to just stay away from him during the move. With her speed, the boys looked like they were standing still. Leham was of course, a blonde-haired and blue-eyed guy with a nice tan. Like Mother like daughter here. You would think that she would be at least a little different from her Mother. Most mother daughters are the exact opposites, but she really was just like her mother. Dan was of course blonde-haired blue-eyed and had the most golden tan. I even think that Leham was like him soul wise as well. They loved their soul mates and would die for them. I know this only because I read Leham's mind. He would never let anything happen to her, as Dan would die instead of me. I could not believe how fast our family was forming. Grady wasn't sure that Kara was his soul mate, only because my son has been so hurt by the girls that he has dated, so he really shies away from the feeling of love towards any woman. I have tried to keep my thoughts away from Kara. I am afraid of learning that she doesn't like him, but that she might like Leham or Jordan instead. But being the mother that I am I could not stop myself. To my amazement, Kara was in a daydream over my son. I was not going to get in the middle the two of them. They would have to figure this out on their own. Leeha and Jordan have been a couple, since they met as Dhampirs. Leeha has the longest brown hair, brown eyes and light skin. She is like my second daughter and is very pretty. She has a heart of gold, but she was one of the girls who had broken my son's heart. For a while, I didn't really care for her anymore. As time went on, I remembered that she has a good heart. But she has just made some bad choices. Leham has brown hair and green eyes, which I believe to have been made a little more of an emerald color due to the change. Kara is a very beautiful young lady with long brown hair, dark skin with baby blue eyes. I have to say we all seemed to fit together so well. I still don't want to let the kids start hooking up so to speak only because of the tasks that we have in front of us right now.

Chapter Eight
The First battle

As our new-found family starts to settle in, I can feel the hunger building in them. I have not felt the need to feed at all, since I killed Hanzi. I have been talking to Dan about taking the family out for dinner. Now I am going to tell the kids about it.

"Ok, so I can feel that you all have been growing hungry as of late. I have taken Grady out on a few little searches for the right place for us to have our first family dinner."

"Yea and I think we found just the right place." Grady is so excited that I took only him to search for the vampyers to have our first family dinner. It made him feel as if only he could do this type of job. Not only could he see into the buildings, but he was the strongest of us all.

"Dan and I have talked about how we should go about going out for our first dinner together. With all of our combined gifts, I don't think that we need to talk about how we will do this. I believe that we need to start thinking on the fly. The remaining eleven are going to attack us at some point, and we need to be able to react without a plan. So tonight we are going out to dinner." Everyone yells and high fives each other. "I will not be eating this evening as I have had a very large meal just nights ago." Laughing I continue to tell them where we are going, and that I will be there to make sure that everyone is safe and that everyone gets to eat. The girls run to change, and the guys start in on who will be the first to kill.

Picture if you can eight of us walking down the street like normal people. We wanted to just take the beginning of the evening slowly, talking together like regular people would. I couldn't have been happier listen to Grady talk to Kara about the things that he likes to do. As he talks to her, she smiles at him. I believe I see her blushing just a little and then her thoughts hit me. She has only been in love once, and he was only dating her to make his ex-girlfriend jealous. When his ex-wanted him back he told her the reason he had been with her. Her heart still hasn't healed from the hurt, he caused her. But Grady makes her feel like she could love him, that he would love her and for her. I knew he would never hurt her. His heart had been hurt as well. But his thoughts were all about her and the dinner we were about to have. Leham walks next to Crysta, and slowly he takes her hand into his. My sweet little girl wanted to pull her hand back, but Leham had the gift of emotions. What I mean is that with him around, he could tap into your emotions. He had tried to use his gift on me after the remaining eleven had come to me. I seem to have some sort of resistance to him. I mean I could feel that he was trying to help me feel less worried. Even so, I needed to feel everything at that moment, so I resisted him. Crysta doesn't really want to resist him. She is just scared that he might hurt her. His touch was something she did want, even though she was fighting her own feelings. Leham has thoughts of only her right now. I would think that he would also be thinking about our first dinner out, but he only has thoughts about her. He didn't want her to get hurt tonight he wasn't going to be away from her side. Well, I knew that they would be fine with their vamps. Then, there were Jordan and Leeha.

They were already grounded in their relationship. Their thoughts were of course about each other and about dinner. They were excited, and their hearts are racing. They can't wait to eat their hunger was more than Crysta's, Grady's or mine. They have not eaten yet. They were afraid of it, but now they know it is what we need, and they can't wait. Then, there was Dan. He has his arm around my waist and keeps me pulled as close to him as he can. He knows that I will not let anything hurt them. Even so, he still is worried about me. He feels that he has waited so long to find me. I feel the same way about him. I just wish I could find a way to block his thoughts. There are moments that he thinks of me, and I want to act on his thoughts. Now is just not the time. The kids are hungry and dinner is right in front of us now.

The building has seven lesser vamps inside. They are not young vamps. They are older. I figured that with all the gifts, we have, taking the older ones would help with the learning about the remaining eleven. As I have told everyone, I want us to just go off of instinct and not over think it. They all need to be able to handle themselves if I am not around.

"Ok I will be right here. Everyone just stay in touch with each other. And remember family try to keep your dinner off of your clothes. I am not sure I have enough stain re mover for everyone." Everyone laughs and say all together . . .

"Oh Mom!" And off they went.

There were three entrances into the building, Crysta and Leham took the back entrance. With Crysta's speed, they were through the door before anyone could see them. Dan went in the front door along with Grady and Kara. Their strength was enough to get through the door as if it wasn't even there. Jordan and Leeha took the side door, seems that Leeha can moves things with her mind as well, so the door was unlocked with no problem. As I watched them, I know that they were not going to run into any problems in there. I enter the building seconds after everyone is in. I am listening to everyone thoughts and feelings to make sure no one is having any trouble. Grady, Dan and Kara are already taking their vamps and feeding. Crysta seems to be playing with her food for a few more seconds then takes him and begins to drain him of his blood. Leham waited to make sure she was ok then just took his vamp, as if he was a rag doll. Jordan and Leeha were the last to eat, but their vamps kept trying to run from them. They were not fast enough for my kids. As everyone was finishing their meals, I sense more thoughts coming at us fast. I link myself to all of my family and show them what I feel. It was like we knew what was happening and in seconds, we were all in the middle of the living room in a circle with our backs to each other. Our hands touch just so I can gather as much energy as I can. I can't see how many vamps there are but there are more than us, I would say at least three times as many. I now have us all linked, so we can all talk without speaking. I tell them that this is a setup and that the Eleven are behind it. They think that if they take us all at once like this that I would be distracted and then one of these sad little lesser vamps might get lucky and kill me. Like everything that has happened to us this goes very fast. I tell them all to get closer together. As we all make our circle tighter I start to let my energy build drawing from everything and everyone around me. This time I begin to glow and so does my family. Dan puts up his shield in front of him which Leeha stretches all around us. Crysta begins to sing to the lesser vamps, and they all seem to slow to a human pace. They were not sure, what was going on I could read from them that the Eleven didn't tell them what they were up against. They thought we were human. But it was too late for them to run. They were told to kill us from their makers, and as I have learned the slaves do as they are told no matter what. We have already weakened them, with Crysta's song, they are unsure of what to do. One by one they try to come at us. They bounce off of Dan's shield like it was a brick wall. I tell my family that I need to get all the vamps together, so I can hit them all at once with my energy. Leeha and Jordan let go of each other, and Leeha keeps Dan's shield around us. Crysta sings them close together. Grady gives all his built up strength to me. I don't know how he did it, but it was a real power boost. As the vamps are all in front of us, I gather up all the energy into one big ball. I tell everyone to focus on my energy and push it towards the vamps with everything we have. And in a second the energy I had was hitting all the lesser vamps like a bomb! When the smoke cleared there was only one vamp left. Grady was on him in second.

"Wait son, don't kill him just yet!"

"I wasn't going to I know what you want from him, just didn't want him getting away." Grady laughs his . . . I know what I am doing laugh. I am talking right to the vamp now.

"I know that the Eleven have sent you after us. And I know that you had no choice but to do what you were told."

"WH . . . what are you?" I can feel and hear the fear that this vamp is feeling. Kara speaks this time.

"We are Dhampirs. We are more powerful than anything you have or every will see. Mikatta is our mother, and she is why all of your friends are dead. We are half vampyer and half human." Kara's emotion was not of fear but of pure anger.

"What do you mean the Eleven? We have twelve masters?" This time Dan had to speak.

"Mikatta has killed your precious Hanzi. And she did that all by herself! So now you know the power that your Masters have sent you up against." He has pride in his voice and power.

"I want you to take a message to your masters. They can send as many of their little slaves to try and kill us, but as you have seen, we will kill them all. So they can send them if they want. We have no problem with killing all of you!"

"Just kill me. If I go back to them, they will kill me anyways."

"No we are not killing you. Mom told you to take the message back, and you are going to do it!" Crysta begins to sing to the vamp, and he stands up and walks out of the building.

"Good thing Mom has that mind reading thing down. That would have taken a little longer than I would have wanted to fight." Jordan is a little shaking by all that has happened. This was his first time fighting and having seen how many vamps that were sent to kill us. He was a little scared.

"No worries Jordan as you can see we are much stronger than they are. I won't let anything happen to you son." I call him son because I can tell he wants me too. His Mother was not a very loving woman. I take Jordan in a hug. I can feel his hum, so I try to take some of it from him. He smiles at me.

"No Mom you have done enough tonight. I can handle the feeling. But thank you!"

"Ok everyone let's get the hell out of here. No need to stand around waiting for something else to happen." Dan tells everyone. At that we all run home. It takes us may be a minute to get there it took us almost thirty minutes just walking there. We get in the house, and everyone starts to get cleaned up. No one is talking to each other at this time. We are all keeping to ourselves as we shower, change and try to gather our own thoughts about what just happened. I stay out of my family's minds right now so that I can focus on my own thoughts. I knew that the Eleven would try something I just didn't think it would have been so soon. I can't believe the true raw power that all of us hold. Leeha using her power to move things to move Dan's shield around us was astonishing. My linking us together seems to give us some kind of super-charged power boost. Crysta's song was so strong that it reached all of the lesser vamps. I knew she could handle at least three with no problem, but there had to be at least forty vamps there. I still can't believe that Grady knew how to transfer his strength to me. It was a marvelous feeling. I could feel how strong he really is. Everyone was so focused on me. Making sure that they gave everything they had to me so that when I had enough energy built up, they could help me send it right where I needed it to go, so I could take out all the lesser vamps. I must say I was a little stunned to see there was one left. But I believe that it was a blessing for us, so we could send our message to the remaining Eleven. Now that everyone has had time to gather their thoughts and are all cleaned up, we gather in the living room. At first, no one says anything. I know they are waiting for me to talk first, but I wanted them to tell me what they thought of everything before I told them what I felt.

"Tonight has shown us that we are definitely tremendously strong. And that we can think on the fly! I think that we have sent a really good message to the Eleven that we are not going to be easy to kill. That doesn't mean that we can go letting our guards down at all. Everyone worked together in a way I don't believe that any of those vamps thought we could do." Dan started the conversation, and sounded like the true father I knew he was inside. He sounded unyielding and proud about the way our family had come together.

"Yea I think they will get the message that we are not going to go down without one hell of a fight." Jordan also had that proud sound in his voice.

"We aren't going down at all. Did you see how much power Mom has? She took out all of them but one. There was at least forty of them, and she just fried them all!" Grady with his nothing can touch us attitude.

"They were just lesser vamps. We knew we could take out the lessers with no problems. The Eleven will be a lot more difficult to handle then that. They only sent those vamps to find out what our gifts were. That was a fact-finding attack. Now they will know what we can throw at them." Crysta did not sound as proud or happy about the whole thing.

"I think you're right sis. Why didn't those vamps know we weren't normal humans? They seemed stunned that we had gifts that we could use against them." Kara was very interested in why this information had not been given to the lesser vamps.

"Ok so the Eleven had their little fact-finding mission, maybe we should have our own little fact-finding mission. We should know what they can do." Leham stated.

"Mom already knows what the Eleven can do. Don't you Mom?" Leeha looks at me like she already knows the answer to her question.

"I do have knowledge of the Eleven. Each one does have remarkable gifts. Ok, let's see, the first one is Belle Burn. She was the vamp that did all the talking when they came for me. She can control anyone's mind. This could really cause problems for us if she can use her gift and make us use our gifts on each other. She can also read minds. And that is probably how they knew where we would be. Marion Arnauld, she can control the animals. Not sure that one is a gift that can cause much difficulty for us, but I wouldn't just over look her. Samuel Pope, now he has the gifts of the elements. This really could mess with me. I draw a lot of my energy from the things around me. I try to draw most of my energy from you guys because it is purer and more powerful. The wind, air, earth and water are also pure energy and give a nice boost. If he finds a way to keep me from doing that it could weaken me. Margravine, now she is nothing but poison. I am not sure how that works. I can't get a full read off of her. It might be that she can block me somehow. Then there is Persia. His only gift is strength. That doesn't mean he couldn't do physical damage to us."

"I want to be the one that takes Persia out!" Grady stands up and smacks his chest like the show of, I am man hear me roar! Everyone let out a little laugh. "What you don't think I can take him?"

"No that is not what everyone is thinking son. It was just your reaction to Persia, and I think the smacking your chest made you look like a caveman. You know this my woman ugh." I tried to lighten the mood a little.

"I just think I would be best at taking him out." Grady sounds a little, pride hurt.

"I know but let me finish telling you all about the rest of them before we start picking which one we each want to kill. OK?"

"Fine."

"Good, now then, there is Angelique Shakespear. Her words are her power. If she speaks it, it is done. So we are going to have to figure out a way to keep her quiet. Moldovia has a very unique gift, he can move in the shadows. That means he can move during the day. All he needs is a small shadow, and he can hide in it. I think that is how they knew that we were going to have our dinner tonight. Michael can put fear into anyone. So we will have to keep our guards up to her. Fear can kill so none of us should let fear in. Thomas Cromwell is a shape shifter. This means he can look like anyone of us. That could really be dangerous for those us who can't read minds. So be aware of each other. We know our family, and we should all be able to tell if one of us is a fake. Ok Giselle Deshoulieies is one I would like to get rid of as soon as possible. She can control the children. That means she can use them against us. I know that none of us want to hurt kids so Leeha your gift will have to help us in moving them out of harm's way if she chooses to use them. The last of the Eleven is Aelfric Flanders. He can blend into his surroundings. The only thing that helps us is me being able to read minds and Grady's gift of being able to see through things. And that is the Eleven pure evil vampyers."

"It sounds like if we have to take them on it would be best to get them in smaller groups. If we try to take them all on at once I do think that we will have casualties." Dan knows what I am thinking and says it for me.

Chapter Nine
Down Time

It has been at least a week since the battle with the vamps. I decided that we would all take some time off from all the killing and what not. I could feel that the kids really wanted to spend some time getting to know each other. And of course I wanted to get to know Dan better! I also needed some time to learn all about this gift of touch I have from Hanzi. I don't want to use it on Dan, but I think it might come in handy with some of the remaining eleven vamps. Grady and Kara were out back on the swing talking about what their likes and dislikes are. Crysta and Leham were in the family room. Crysta was doing her best not to show how much she liked Leham of course she wasn't really doing that good of a job at it. Leham's heart, I believe he wears on his sleeve for her. He has already told her that he is in love with her, and that he doesn't want her to say it to him until she really means it. He knows that she was hurt, and he handles her in the most compassionate way I have ever seen a young man accomplish. Since Jordan and Leeha already have gotten to know each other they just sit and watch some TV and do the cuddling thing. Their thoughts are on each other, and I hear Jordan's thoughts. He wants to ask Leeha to marry him. I sit up and gasp for air!

"Mikatta what is it?" Dan asks.

"Oh, oh nothing . . . it's nothing." I lean back into his arms and try not to look so worried.

"Ok remember what my gift is babe? Tell me, what has you so worried? Please, trust me."

"Sorry, I am just not sure I should tell you. I really need to stay out of the kid's heads when we are not fighting.

Hearing their thoughts about each other is not something any Mother should have the gift to do. Jordan wants to ask Leeha to marry him."

"No he can't! They are two young for that." Dan's reaction to this surprises me.

"Dan Leeha is twenty-four years old, and Jordan is twenty-six. That is not too young. And why on earth are you acting this way about the two of them? You have only known them for what four months? You had to know that they had feelings for each other."

"I'm sorry it is just that I feel like they are my kids. I knew that they liked each other. But I didn't know it had gotten to love. I don't want them to get hurt, that's all."

"Dan dear. I have known Leeha for more than half her life, and yes there was a time I wasn't very happy with her. I know her heart is good though. She really does love Jordan. Most of the time they only think about each other. They wonder what it would be like to have a family . . ." I stop dead in my sentence. Oh God, could we have children? And if we did what would they be? We need a family meeting and we need it right now. I link myself to everyone and tell them in the living room RIGHT NOW!

"Mom is everything ok?" Jordan is the one to ask the question, and I wonder if he knows I was listening to his thoughts.

"Yes, I think we really need to talk about something that has just hit me. I know that we all seem to fit together rather nicely. It is apparent that we have coupled up. I, being Mom, had a thought about something that I really think we all need to think about. At some point, one or more of us is going to . . . well let's just say that sex is something that seems to be in all of our futures." I get a lot of groans and oh God Moms at this. "I know no one likes to talk to their parents about sex. I think for us, it is something that we should do, not because I don't think that you all shouldn't have it. But because of what might come out of it. Children and I have no idea what our children would be. Do we have the right to bring babies into a world that is like this, and to be like us? What if they are full vampyer and not half like us? I know the way that each of you is feeling about each other. I am not dense to our reality here. I want everyone to be happy and safe. So if anyone thinks that getting pregnant is something they want to really do, then we really must talk about it." For a moment, no one says anything they all sit there thinking about what I have just said.

"You are right Mom this is something I don't think that we have really put a lot of thought into yet. And yes I do want to have kids. Now that you have brought it up, I don't know . . . What if they are evil?" Leeha begins to tear up at the thought of not being able to have a child. I go to her and hold her tight to me.

"I do not believe that any of our children would be evil sweet heart. If they were full vamp, we could not let them live. Because they would only want to feed from humans, and I just can't have that. So I think that if anyone here is to try this . . . it should be Dan and I." Even Dan gives a gasp at what I have just said.

"Why should you have to go through that my love? You are too wonderful a mother. How could you handle killing your own child if it were evil? I don't think you should have to go through that kind of pain my sweet."

"Dan, I have six wonderful children sitting right here with me. I will have them for the rest of all our long-lived lives. I am the only one who could do this. Would you truly want Leeha, Kara or Crysta to have to lose their first child if they are full vampyers? Is that fair? I don't believe so. I don't want them to go through losing a child."

Once again, the room was very quit. I know that I can listen to all of their thoughts but the only one I am listening to is Leeha. Because I believe that she has more that she wants to say but is keeping it to herself. Then I listen to Dan. He wants to have a baby with me. It would make him so happy if he could have his own child. And he really wants me to be the mother. Dan stands up and then gets down on one knee . . .

"Mikatta Hope from the moment that you have come into my life, I have wanted nothing more than to be able to spend the rest of it with you. I love you! There isn't one part of me that doesn't want to be with you. Would you please do me the honor of being my wife?"

I think I must have lost my breath because my head started to spin a little. Everyone was in shock. No one thought that Dan would ask me to be his wife so soon after his had just left him. Grady and Crysta both stand up and come to sit beside me. They both wrap their arms around me and hug me tight.

"We know that this is not something that you have thought about since Dad passed away Mom. Dan really will be there for you forever. He truly loves you. I can tell that he does. I know I was against him and you to begin with, but I have watched him stare at you and the look on his face is the one I believe I must have as I stare at Kara. So, you have my blessings Mom to marry this remarkable Man." Grady says all of this and does not once stammer. He says it with pride and confidence. This is something I didn't believe my son would ever say to me, that I could marry another man.

"Grady is right Mom. Dan is so right for you. I have seen it. I have also seen children." Everyone looks right at my daughter with the same face.

"What have you seen Crysta? Are they like us or are they . . . ?" Leeha can't finish the question.

"All I can see is a baby. One baby and I cannot see past its birth. I do not know who the baby is born to or what it becomes. I get the feeling that the child is born to Mom. And if anyone would be able to handle this child it would be her. Look, you deserve to let yourself love Dan Mom. He wants you to be with him until the end of us. Dan I give you my blessing to marry my mother."

I don't know what to say, I am having trouble thinking. I do love this man that I do know. Only, I don't think I could live through losing another husband. But Dan is no normal man. He is a very powerful Dhampir! He is just like me and the rest of my family. What did I think that Dan would want to just be together and have kids without being married to me? I knew him better he has wanted to marry me.

"YES!" And all at once, the room is loud with "Hell yea" and "Congratulations." The girls screaming and jumping up and down and lots of hugging and shaking hands.

Now my daughters have taken to planning the wedding. I am letting them do all of that, so I can focus on any vamps that might come after us. We have been talking about whether or not we should invite any real family to the wedding. I mean my parents are still alive. Dan lost his parents to a car accident. However, I am worried, if it will be safe to have them close by us with everything that has been happening. So I deiced that for our family's safety that it should just be the eight of us for now. As the girls are sitting around making all the plans, Jordan comes into the room and asked if he could please talk to Leeha alone.

"I wanted to do this the other day but everything just got so chaotic so fast I didn't have the chance to do it." Jordan gets on one knee and holds up a little black box with a beautiful engagement ring and says . . . "Leeha you know that we are soul mates, and that we are truly meant to spend the rest of our lives together. So I am asking you to make me the happiest Dhampir in the whole world and be my wife?" Leeha drops to her knees in tears.

"You would be making me the happiest Dhampir if you would have me as your wife. Yes! I will marry you."

I didn't mean to hear them but well, you know me by now I am the Mom, and I just can't help myself. I let out a little squeak, and Dan asks me what is wrong.

"Nothing is wrong dear, Jordan and Leeha will be getting married as well." I smile as I tell this to Dan to show that I am happy for them. Because I know he is not as thrilled with the idea of them getting married.

"And you are ok with this I take it?" He asks me.

"Yes I am. They are adults, and they are in love. They know that they are soul mates and there should be no reason that they should not be married." I say this with all of my heart so that Dan can really understand the meaning of the two of them being together.

"Well if you think that it is ok, then I will support them as well. You know how I really feel about it. I will just be sure to make a good show of being happy for them."

"In time my love you will be truly happy for them, you will see." I softly kiss him and wrap my arms around his neck. It is a good thing we are already in our room. He has waited too long to have me. I want him as badly as he wants me. I tell him . . .

"I really would like to wait until our wedding night, if you think that you can hold on that long? I don't mean that we can't fool around, but I want it to be on our wedding night." I am scared of his answer and I stay out of his mind.

"I will honor you in any way you ask my love. But I am going to take you up on the fooling around you stunning Dhampir you!" He tosses me on the bed and kisses me with more passion this time. He honored me in the best way he could.

It turned out that we decided to have a double wedding. We decided to have just us and a pastor to marry us. I do not believe that I have ever felt more magnificent than I did standing there taking my vows with Dan. Knowing that our life together would be long, but not without the tough spots. Crysta was my maid of honor, and Grady was Dan's best man. When the pastor said "I know pronounce you man and wife" I let out a laugh, I couldn't hold it in knowing that we were not simple men and women in this room. It then came "You may kiss your bride" and I was floating. He was my husband now, and I was his wife, something I did not believe would ever happen to me again. Leeha and Jordan's wedding followed and was just as wonderful. When the pastor left finally all of us let loose. Now we could dance and really be ourselves. I can't remember a more fantastic day. Everyone was happy we seem to have forgotten about the Eleven and the lessers.

My wedding night was like nothing I could ever explain. Being what we were, we felt things on a heighten level. I believe at some point we were really floating.

I knew the moment that I was pregnant. I knew it was a boy. And the rate of growth was going to be quick. I didn't tell Dan right away. I still wasn't sure what the baby was or was going to be. I just wanted to lie in his arms and let the night be ours. Morning came, and I couldn't hide the bump in my belly from him.

"How is that possible? I mean you look as if you are at least six months along!"

"I told you that I had no idea how this was going to work. I think at this rate the baby will be born tomorrow. I don't want the kids to know until we know what it is. Please just tell everyone I just want to spend this time with you." My voice is shacking at this point. Dan can see that I need to do this alone with him.

We spend the day in our room watching the baby grow. Dan talks to my stomach telling the baby that it was good and that in our family, it would be a good Dhampir. I wanted everything that he was telling the baby to be true. My heart longed for it all to be true. It then came, the ripping pain in my stomach. I covered my face with a pillow so the kids wouldn't hear my screams, but I knew they would.

"Mom! Mom! What is going on are you ok? Let us in. Dan let us in, we can help. Please don't let her go through this without us!" Crysta pleaded with us, I tell Dan to let them in.

Again, I feel the ripping pain, like something was trying to tear its way out of me. This was not the way a baby was born. This child was going to tear its way out of my stomach. I didn't want it this way, so I link myself to the baby like I linked myself to the others. I try talking to the baby. "This is your Mom and this is not the way you should come out of me. There is a better and easier way than hurting me. Let me show you how to come out." Almost as if the baby really heard me the pain stopped.

"It hears you Mom. Just tell the baby what to do and I think you'll be fine." Crysta is holding my hand and has linked herself to me this time. I tell the baby how it should really be born, and in like seconds the little boy was in Dan's arms wrapped in a towel. Then came that beautiful baby cry. Everyone breathed for a moment, but still we were not sure if this child was a full vamp or if it was a Dhampir like us. I tell Dan to give me the baby, he hands me our son. I touch his amazing face, and then I feel a tingle rush through me, I begin to cry because I can see what he is. He is my son and he is just like Dan and I. He is a Dhampir.

"He is ours! He is just like us. If I couldn't link with him, he would have torn his way out of me, and I don't know if that would have killed me or not. So if any of the rest of you girls get pregnant I will have to be there with you so that I can link with the baby to help it be born the right way."

"Wow he is amazing Mom, what are you going to name him?" Kara asks.

"I am not the one naming him" I laugh, "He has told me what his name is. Meet your little brother Anthony."

"Can I hold him?" Leeha is the first to ask. I know it is because she wants to be able to have a child as soon as possible.

"Of course but I think I need to feed him, get him cleaned up while you girls go buy the things this little guy will be needing."

"Oh yea we can't have him running around naked!" Kara pulls the girls, and they are off. I was hoping that the human half of my son would want to eat breast milk because I could feel that I was full and ready to feed him. He went straight to the breast. But he wasn't just getting milk, I could tell that there was blood mixed in with it when I wiped his mouth. It seems my body knew what he needed and can give him both. All of this was coming at us so fast I wasn't sure what to do. When he was full I got up and cleaned him off. The girls were back in a flash with all the things that we would need for little Anthony. As the girls took over I took a shower and just cried. How can this be, a baby Dhampir? If he only took a day to grow inside me how fast would he grow up? It is time that we move our home out of the city. This wasn't going to be something that we could explain to friends and neighbors. Not to mention our family. I knew what we had to do, and now I had to tell the family!

Chapter Ten
Time to Change

Everyone was sitting in the bedroom playing with their new baby brother. He seemed so happy just to be with us. He seemed like any normal baby at his age, for the moment. They were all laughing and smiling. How is that we have been able to handle everything that has come at us so well? I mean it has only been six months from when all of this all first started. I don't think even one of us has not wanted what was happening to us to happen. We just went with it as it came at us. So why did I feel that what I was about to tell everyone would change the way we were all feeling right now? I had to do it, there was no other way for us to continue like we are. Not now with Anthony being born.

"I have something I need to tell everyone, and I don't think you're going to like what I have to say. So please just listen to me first and when I am done then you may speak." Everyone was quiet and looked at me with that you know we will do whatever you want Mom face. "Ok Now that we have little Anthony, I think we are going to have to change the way we live, or should I say the place we live. There is no way of knowing how fast he will grow. He was only conceived last night. There is just no way to explain him to people. I am sure he will look like he is two in about a week. That isn't the worst of what I have to say. I think it is time for us to take ourselves out of our families lives as well. And that means we have to be dead to them!" I am quite now because I am not really sure how we are going to be able to pull that one off.

"Your right, we have already brought to much attention to ourselves living here. I am sure the neighbors think that we are all insane. We never sleep and we are always home, unless we are out feeding. And your right with the baby, well there really isn't anyway we will be able to hide that from normal people. I have thought of an idea, of how we can take ourselves out, so to speak." Grady was right there with me on everything, even the way I had thought of to make it look like we had died. "A house fire would do the trick. The only thing we need is bodies, and that isn't even going to be hard. All we have to do is find some vamps that look sort of like us and use their bodies."

"You have thought about this a lot Grady." Kara looks up at him.

"Well yea, sort of, I mean I knew that at some point we were going to have make it look like we were dead to our family at least. So the best way would be a fire."

"Before all of that can be done we need to find a place in the country where there are no other humans around. Get new identities and still track the vamps. Wow we really need to find a way to have some real down time." I laugh, and so does everyone else. "Money isn't a problem for us, but we will have to find someone that can get us the new ids."

"I know where we can go to live!" Dan pipes up all happy like. "My family, which, by the way, is only me now, owns this really big ranch that hasn't been used in years, only because it has just been me. No one ever goes up that way. And the nearest neighbor is twenty miles away."

"See now I knew you were the most wonderful man in the world." I kiss my new husband and hand our son off to him. "Ok so I guess that means we all know what we need to do now. We need to find us some bodies and start getting the ranch ready for us to move into." The part about the bodies came out so easy that I had to laugh a little to it. Ok woman, just remember that you are not a killer and that the only bodies you would ever talk like that about are vampyers.

It is remarkable the way that we work as one when things need to be done quickly. Everyone found something that needed to be done and started working on it. And I was right about little Anthony. He was growing at a very rapid rate. So we needed to get things done now. The kids would run back and forth between the ranch and the house at night. The ranch was just about ready for us to move in. Jordan and Leham had found just the right vamps for us to use as our body doubles. I decided that I wanted all the kids to take Anthony to the ranch and stay there with him the night that we would have our little house fire. I felt that, Dan, and I could handle this on our own.

You know that feeling that you get when you know that something is about to happen, but you're not sure if it is a good or a bad thing? Well, the day of our little plan I got that feeling. I didn't say anything to the family, mostly because I thought I was just over worried about being split up for a little while. So the kids took Anthony to the ranch, and Dan and me, went off to get our body doubles.

How stupid could I have been to not think that Belle didn't know what was going on with us? She has the power to control minds, and to read them as well.

The eight vamps were still sleeping, it wasn't quit sunset yet. I was very hungry, due to all the feeding that I had been doing for Anthony. So killing them before they awoke was no problem. As we finished our last feeds, I felt the other vamps closing in on us.

"Dan! It's a trap there are at least twenty of them coming." Dan puts his shield up and has learned to move it around us, including our dead body doubles. I am building up all the energy that I can with what little there was around me. They are trying to break through Dan's shield, but he has fed and the shield holds strong. I feel I can build no more energy, and I let it loose on the vamps. It only hits about a third of them.

"I want to fight them, it will be easier and I won't waste all my power." I tell Dan this because I now have the feeling that the kids need us. Dan lowers his shield and we easily take out the remaining vamps. I feed on some to gain more energy. We grab our doubles and race back to the house.

"Grady they are coming! The vamps they know we are here. We need to protect Anthony, they were sent to get him!" Crysta is terrified. She can see what is happening to Dan and me, and now sees what is coming for them.

"Everyone in the basement NOW!" Grady hurries everyone down to the basement where he feels he can keep them away from Anthony. "Crysta, stay with Anthony, the rest of us will act as a wall between you. Mom and Dan will know what is happening and will get to us as soon as they can. Until then we can hold them off."

It was as if they were an army of ants. They came at my children with such force. At first, they fought with no problems. Grady's strength was unyielding and would not let one vamp pass. Crysta sang to confuse them as the others fought. The vamps were so many. Anthony stands up and turns and looks at Crysta. He moves closer to his brothers and sisters, raises his hands and his eyes begin to glow a deep purple. Suddenly, Grady, Kara, Leeha, and Leham were moved back away from the vamps. Then like nothing they had seen before, Anthony wills all the vamps to be gone! And just like that they are all dust.

I knew the minute he had done this because it was, as if he had drawn power from me to do it. He linked to me somehow and pulled my energy to him from all those miles. I dropped to my knees I had no strength at that moment. Dan rushes to me.

"My Love what it is? What has happened?"

"Our son, he took my power, but not to hurt me. They were being attacked by vamps. The kids they were holding them off, but there were way too many of them. Anthony he . . . he has a gift. He can project what he wants onto anyone. He wanted them gone, so they just turned to dust. He needed more power than his little body had, so he linked to me and took mine." I can barely breath. I feel as if I am almost human again. "Get the bodies to the house I will rest for a little bit." Dan doesn't wait he does what I ask. He knows that we can't wait any longer to finish our plan.

The fire trucks arrive and try to put out the flames, but we have made sure that they would not be able to do so until the bodies were burned beyond recognition. We made it seem as if there was a small gas leak, and someone started a fire in the fireplace. I was sad watching the home that we had made go up in flames. As soon as I knew we were ok and that our plan had worked Dan, and I left for the ranch. I was still very weak so Dan carried me. The trip was short, but I felt as if my whole life was moving for the first time in slow motion. I watched the trees go by, and looked at the stars in the sky. What had happened tonight? I hold on tight to my husband who returns my hold. I see the ranch in front of us and feel relief that we are finally here, so I can see that my family is truly ok. As Dan brings me inside the kids rush to my side, then he sets me gently on the couch.

"Mom, are you ok what happened to you?" Leeha has tears in her eyes as she sees me look so weak.

"I did it to her." Anthony speaks. These aren't the first words that we have heard from him but it is the first time he has spoken like he is an adult. "I needed her power. She is the most powerful of us and to make them all go away, I needed her power." He walks up to me, places his small hand on my check. "I am sorry mommy! I didn't want anyone to get hurt. I should have asked you before I did it. I promise I won't do it again without asking." I pick up my son and hold him as close as I can and I begin to cry.

"No son! You do not need to be sorry for what you did. You did the right thing. You protected our family, and that is what we do. I was so afraid that they were going to hurt all of you, and I couldn't do anything to stop them. I was so far away, but you pulled the power from me even from that distance, how?"

"You are my mommy, and I am every part of you. You can do the same with anyone of us. You just don't. You only use a little bit of our powers to help you. I didn't mean to take all your power, but I am still learning how to use my gift." He smiles as he kisses my cheeks a whole bunch of times. I hold on so tight to my youngest son. All of my kids come to my side and hold onto me. Like a wave of water washing over me, I feel all my power come crashing back. I pick them all up and swing them around.

Once again, our family has shown that we are very powerful. I will not forget about Belle's power again. She can read minds, and we need to find a way to block her from us. I don't know how but we have to keep what we are doing from them. Now that the eleven know about Anthony. I know what they want. They can't have children, but we can. They want our babies to use for themselves. Oh God, please help me keep my family safe from them! Crysta has seen what Belle has in mind for us, she doesn't really want us dead now. She wants to try and breed with us to see if the combination would bring forth a child of evil. We will never let this happen. For now I believe that we have a little time to ourselves. It is time to try and settle into our new home. The kids have found their rooms and have settled in quit well. Anthony looks as if he is at least six-years old now, and he has only been alive for two weeks. Leeha and Jordan have decided that they will wait to have a child until we have gotten a little firmer grasp on our new lives. I don't blame them this is not what I had wanted for us. I was really hoping that this move, this change would be a good thing for us. Right now we just need to regroup. We need to prepare the ranch so that we can be ready for the next attack. So that for a little while we might be able to relax and enjoy our renewed lives. I know, how can I think that our lives had been renewed? Because I know that I had given up on love and the chance of having a happy and big family. Now I have both and this is our time of renewal!

Dan has taken to putting in a security system all around the ranch. There isn't a part of the ranch that isn't covered. We can see everything, he even put up sensors all around that will set off if anything comes close to the ranch! Leeha is making good use of her time with Anthony, she is teaching him how to control his gift of projection. Leeha has learned very quickly how to control her gifts, so of course we knew she would be the best to teach her nephew how to control his. Plus, maybe they can find a way not to drop me to my knees when he does need to use my power. Grady has been working with the rest of the family, going through training so to speak. He wants everyone to know how to work together with our powers against the mass amounts of vamps that we will be up against. I have been looking into what I have seen about Belle, and what she wants from us now. She wants us alive now, but it is at a cost. We would be their little baby makers. I haven't told the family about what I know. I don't what to tell them at this point. We have so much to deal with right now. I have a son that is only three weeks old and looks like he is seven-years old. He is smart, the things that he knows at his age! He tells me . . .

"Mommy you gave me all the knowledge when I was inside you. I told you we are forever linked, and I can draw your energy from you. Just as you can draw from me, only you don't. Why don't you try to use my gifts Mommy?"

"You are still a baby to me Anthony. I don't know what my linking and using your powers would do to you. I will not put you in any danger. We still don't know everything about you, how old you will become, what other gifts you have? These are things that only time will tell us. I am willing to wait if it means not hurting you my darling." I put him on my lap and kiss his beautiful blonde head. He looks so much like his father. Every day he looks more and more like Dan. He hugs me so tight I can't believe the power that this little Dhampir has already. And the love that he holds inside for us.

The ranch is finally ready for us to try and relax in. The boys have made a recreation room to play around in, and a room where they can practice their powers and their fighting abilities. The girls have fixed up the kitchen and the sunroom so we can have a place to just sit around and have a lot of girl talk. Behind all this, thinking, we still had the Eleven waiting in the background. But for now I wanted us to have this time, this time of being a happy family!

Chapter Eleven
Our Turn

There have been no attacks by the vamps for three weeks now. I am not relaxed about this in the least. So I bring the family together to talk about what I think we need to do.

"We have been attack free for three weeks now, and I know that everyone is feeling really good about that. But I need to tell you something that I have been keeping from you. Belle wants Anthony. And not just him, she wants us all alive, so she can try to breed with us to see if they can have babies with us. That is why the attacks have stopped. She is looking for a way to get to us and take us alive. I don't want to sit around here and just wait for that to happen."

"I will not be a sitting duck for that bitch. I say we start taking out their little vamps and weed them out a bit!" Grady has that anger in him that I am always afraid of. "There is no way I will just sit around and let them come for our family."

"Nor will I son. Mikatta, why didn't you tell us this sooner? This is not something you should have kept from us. The only thing that we have that the Eleven don't is our love and trust for each other. If you keep things from us then the trust part is no longer there!" Dan's words cut through my heart like a knife!. I try to hold back the tears that I feel coming. I didn't mean to lie to them, but they were all so happy, and I just wanted them to have that, to be happy for just a little time.

"Dan, don't you dare talk to my mother that way! She is only trying to let us have some happiness. And if you ever think for one second that she doesn't trust us then maybe you should leave." Crysta is in Dan's face and is yelling at this point. "She has done everything that she can to keep this family together and safe. She has even given you a son, who could have killed her. And you stand there and accuse her of being dishonest? Maybe you don't love her the way you claim."

"Crysta, please it is ok I know that I should have told you all sooner. I just wanted us to have a little time of being happy and a family before we had to go through another huge battle. I am sorry!"

"No mom Crysta is right, Dan, I love you like a father, but don't you ever doubt my Mother again. She has done everything so that we would be safe and together as a family. If you don't know that by now, then . . . ." Leeha can't finish what she wants to say because she really doesn't want him to leave. I couldn't believe that they all were feeling as hurt as I was from Dan's words. Dan looked as if he had been kicked in the stomach.

"Stop it, all of you! Dan, do you really feel as if I have lied to you?" He hangs his head. I have not read my family's mind in weeks, and I read his thoughts. He does feel as if I have hid something from him.

"In a way yes, I know that you love us, and that you are doing everything that you can to keep us safe and happy. I do wish you would have told us about Belle's plans."

"That is fair, but I didn't tell you to hide it from you or to lie to you. I am sorry that you feel that way!" I can't hold it in any longer. I get up and run from the room. I run outside and I just keep running. My heart is ripping in two. The one person I thought knew me and thought would understand me, was the one I had hurt the most. I should have told him. I can't change that I didn't tell him, and I can't change the way he feels. I don't want to stop running, but I know that I shouldn't go far. I stop and sit on a broken tree. In seconds, Dan is at my feet.

"I am so sorry I had no right to say those things to you Mikatta. I do know you better than that. I am such an ass!" He puts his head in my lap, and I feel his pain. "You are everything to me, and I know that you feel the same for me. I let my mouth open before my head gave it permission. Please, please forgive me for being such an idiot? I beg you my love."

"I think we both need to say we are sorry. I should have trusted you with what I knew. I truly just wanted everyone to have a little down time. I am sorry I did not trust you with what I knew." He lifts his head, takes my face in his hands and kisses me. I can feel everything that he wanted to share with me at that moment. I think that he knew my heart needed to be repaired. The electricity went through me and right to my heart. It felt as if he was trying to fix what he knew he had broken.

"Come back to the house with me please, I think that you had more to say and I, and my big mouth, stopped you."

"Of course I will come back to the house with you." Dan picks me up and holds me in his arms and carries me back to ranch. He holds on to me so tight, as if he felt I might slip away from him. I returned the hold on him. I don't want to lose him. Nor do I want to hurt him by making him feel that I don't trust him. I whisper in his ear . . .

"I love you Dan. I don't ever want to hurt you, and I don't want to lose you. I am so sorry I didn't tell you what I knew about Belle." Dan stops dead in his tracks. He Looks me right in the eyes and tells me . . .

"You will NEVER lose me my love! And the only one who needs to apologize is me. I should never doubt you. You are the only person that I know I can trust. Everything you have ever done should have already proven that you would never lie to me. And that you do everything for this family. I was a fool to say those things to you. I will never disrespect you like that ever again my love. Please forgive me?"

"It is the past now, and I will never bring it up again."

The kids were all on edge as they watch Dan carry me back into the house. I hear them all asking did he make it right.

"Dan and I are fine. And yes we both have made it right!" Grady had already thought of the plans that we should use to go about our little vamp killing spree! "Yes Grady you should tell everyone what you have come up with."

"Cool, thanks Mom I really did want to be the one to be in command!" He laughs deep and pounds on his chest. My son, the great Tarzan of Dhampirs.

Grady lays out his plans to the family. He even has every detail down to the point. He wants us to take them out in slow bunches. Weaken them by taking out there slaves. He and Jordan will go out in search of the lesser vamps.

Because he can see through walls, he will know how many there are and what the inside layout is, so we can go in and take them quickly. Then they come back, and we all go together and feed as we kill the lesser vamps. He is very proud that he has come up with this plan all on his own. And I am just as proud of him.

"Do I get to come?" Anthony asks in a firm voice.

"Well little man, you have shown that you can hold your own. As long as you don't wipe out Mom, yea you get to come. Besides I think you might need to feed as well." Dan scoops our son into his arms as he tells him that he gets to have his first kill. Now as the Mother of this child I don't feel the same way. I know he needs to feed, but I do not want him in harm's way. I know he has his own power, and I can't keep him from it forever. He seems happy that he gets to come along. I can't tell if he is happy because he will be with us, or because he gets to have his first taste of vampyer blood. I am worried that he is too young for all this. I am trying not to show how scared this is making me at this point. Grady is ready to take Jordan on their first vamp finding mission. We all wish them luck, and I link myself to both, of them giving them all the help that I can at this point. They head into the city, and I am listening to their thoughts, both are excited and can't wait to find the vamps. They know the minute they do we will come to them and take out the vamps. Jordan can smell a vamp like nothing I have ever seen. They follow his noise and find a small loft with about ten vamps. Grady looks through the walls to see what the layout is, and if we can enter the building and kill them fast. I am trying my best to block Grady and Jordan's thoughts to just me. I am trying to keep what they are up to out of Belle's mind. She has been able to read into ours and know what we are up to. I know that we can block her, just not really sure I am doing it. Grady tells me that we can take the vamps with no problem.

"They are ready for us." We all start off after them. Crysta has to run slower just to stay with us. She laughs at us calling us slow pokes. Running through the county side at night is very relaxing. I can smell the trees, flowers, and even the dirt smells good to me. Everything looks different when you are running at the speed we do, but we can see things like any normal person would as they are running. The evening sky is clear tonight and the moon is bright, not that we need it to see. We reach Grady and Jordan, and they are so ready to take out the vamps. I feel the energy that they are building up. Anthony steps next to me and takes my hand.

"I will stay close to you Mommy. I promise I won't get hurt in there." My son can tell that I need him safe and by my side.

"Thank you son." I hold tight to his hand, and we all surround the building. Of course, the vamps are on the top floor. But that is not a problem for us. We leap onto the sides of the building and climb up to the loft. At the same time, we all break through the windows. With Anthony's hand still in mine we advance on the vamps. Crysta starts to sing and I tell her to stop.

"Grady would like just a little bit of a fight tonight." I laugh as I say this, because Grady is already fighting three of the vamps and has all of them on the floor. Anthony and I take two vamps that are trying to get out the door. I grab one at the same time Anthony takes the others foot and pulls him back to him. We pin the two against the wall, and I tell Anthony that he may go first.

"Don't worry Mommy, I am only doing it because I am hungry." And with that, my baby sinks his fangs into the vamp and begins to drain it of all its blood. I am worried that he may not be able to drink all the blood, but he has no problem filling himself with the vamps blood. The female I have pinned against the wall looks at me and begs . . .

"Please don't kill me. I can tell you what you want to know about the masters!" For a moment, I think I might let her live. Then I read her mind. She knows nothing that I do not already know.

"To bad that wasn't true, and it is too bad I am very hungry." I sink in and drain her of every last drop of her blood. Crysta has had a little bit of a fight with her vamp, and he has pushed her against the wall. Jordan leaps on top of the vamp and knocks him to the floor. Crysta pounces on top of the male. My daughter is so angry that she rips into this male with such power, I almost worry that she is allowing the anger that she was feeling taking over her emotions. But I feel her calm as she is finishing her vamp. Grady has taken three vamps to the ground and has eaten only one. He saves the other two for Kara and Leeha, who so lady like sit on top of their victims and drink nice and slow. Dan is very hungry and decides he will be drinking from two of the vamps that we have found this evening. My husband feels he needs a little extra boost to keep up with his wife. I laugh to myself as I read him. Jordan has to chase after his vamp again after letting him go to help Crysta. But he catches her on the stairs and tosses her right back up into the loft. Leaping on top of her, he drains her as she slaps and kicks to get away from him. Anthony and I stand and watch as the family finishes off their dinner. I sweep him up into my arms and hold him so tight and so close to my heart. He wraps his arms around my neck and nuzzles his head in, as if he was going to go to sleep in my arms. Then I feel the hum that is going through his body, and know why he needs to be so close to me. I use my energy to sooth him, taking away some of the high that he is feeling.

Back at the ranch we all sit in the family room. Anthony is still holding on tight to me. Dan sits behind me holding us both. We are all pleased with our outing and that Belle did not send more vamps after us.

"Leeha dear I think that you and Dan need to work on using his shield to block Belle from our minds." I said this out of nowhere and they all look at me, as if I have lost my mind.

"How on earth would that even work Mom? Dan's shield keeps the vamps from touching us. How can it block our minds from her?" Leham asks.

"It is something that Anthony said to me the day he stole my powers from me. He said that we are family, and we all can share our powers. I think that with Leeha's power and Dan's combined, they can find a way to shield each of our minds." Anthony lifts his head and says . . .

"I can help with that Mommy. I can project what I want onto anyone that I want to. I will project Dan's shield onto all of our minds. But I will need Leeha to move his shield into smaller pieces. So I can wrap it around each one of us separately."

"It sounds good but how can you hold it there for the length of time that we will need?" Jordan asks the question that everyone else is thinking.

"They won't have to. I will." I tell him. "I will hold the link between all of us, and in doing so I can hold what they do. I will need to feed more often than normal. But with Grady's plan, I think that isn't going to be a problem."

"It will work." Crysta says. "She won't be able to see us anymore. Do it!" The four of us each link and Dan pushes out his shield. Leeha breaks it into nine pieces. Anthony projects it onto each one of us. I hold them in place with a very small amount of energy. It is easier than I thought I would be. Crysta smiles and nods, we did it. She can't read our minds anymore. Finally, I can stop worrying about her knowing our every move. I know she isn't the only one that we need to worry about, but for now I am very happy that she does not know our every move. Anthony cuddles back up to me.

"Mommy you are very special, and if we didn't have you, we would no longer exist."

"Why do you say that Anthony?" I can't believe that he would say something like this.

"Because you have good, pure energy inside you. Only you can control it. God gave it to you. It is why you are who you are. God knows what is in your heart and he needs you to help him." I sat there holding my son and cried. I knew what he was saying to be true. I could feel it every time I used the energy that was inside me. We were not just made by the vampyers we were also made by God!

Chapter Twelve
Taking Control

Everyone is quite as I hold my youngest to me and we begin to glow. I feel all the good that is in him, and all the good that is in me. The rest of the family gathers close and we all hold onto each other. This is the first time that we have even thought that we were made of good. We have thought that because the blood packets are what turned us into what we are, that we were made from evil. My son knows things that we do not. When he speaks these things, we all feel the truth in them. The room is full of our good energy. We know that what we are, it is something that has to fight this evil. We also know that we can be killed by the original vampyers. Our gifts were given to us because of what was in our hearts when we were changed. Now we know why we were truly made.

We have had time to rest, and regroup from what we have learned of ourselves. Grady is ready to go out again, one because he is antsy and two because I need to feed. So he and Jordan go out again in search of lesser vamps. The others do not need to feed so this mission is for me only. They need to find something for me to eat so I can have the energy to keep our shields up. I follow behind a ways so that I can enjoy the evening air. Jordan finds three vamps that are close. They are not in a building, but they are out in the streets walking, hunting for their own food. I catch up quickly. These vamps are very old. They smell the human in us and believe that we might be their next meal. I know how hungry I am and feel the energy start to build inside.

"Mom please, let me fight for you. You need to feed, save your energy." Grady can see that I am ready to kill, but knows that I should save my energy. Jordan stands in front of me as well. He holds his hand around my waist, this way he can push me out of the way if he feels that I need to be moved. I try to move his hand but he has a strong grip.

"Mom this way I can bring you to them, please let us do this for you?" Jordan pleads with me.

"Alright, you may do the fighting. Only because I need to save my energy." I don't think I could fight tonight I am so hungry. Keeping the shields up has taken a lot of my energy. Grady approaches the three by himself.

"Nice night we are having wouldn't you say?" Grady tries talking to the vamps. He just wants to play with them a little.

"It is not going to be a good one for you human."

"See now I was trying to be nice about this, but you had to go and be all rude. I am so not a human. I am a Dhampir, and you are my mother's dinner for the evening!" At that Grady plowed all three of the vamps down. He holds one up in the air and with his foot holds one on the ground. Jordan grabs the third and holds him in front of me.

"I would like you to meet my Mother. Her name is Mikatta Hope. She is the Mother of all good, and you are her appetizer." I sink my fangs deep in the vamps neck. I have never been this hungry before. I drain the vamp in seconds.

"Heads up." Grady tosses the next vamp to Jordan.

"I will call you her main course. I have to say she is very hungry this evening so who knows." Jordan is enjoying toying with these vamps. I sink my fangs into the next vamp, drinking just as fast as the last.

"Ok you, I believe you shall be dessert. If she feels full that is?" Grady laughs, as he can see that I am very hungry. This one is older than the other two, as I start to drink, I see flashes of his maker. Persia, he is the strongest of the Twelve original vampyers. Jordan has to hold tight to this vamp. He is strong and fights me.

"Hey now don't be rude, she isn't done yet." Grady is there holding the vamp as well to make it easier for me to feed. I finish this one off, and feel almost full. I now have seen Persia, and as I have found in the past, that means he has seen me as well. I know that the shield is holding so that Belle can't read us, but Persia will know me now. He will come for me. My hunger is still there, and I need more food.

"Grady I am still hungry. I need more."

"Jordan can you find us more?"

"Give me just a minute, and I will!" Jordan knows that I need to feed to keep up the block, so he quickly moves to find me more food. He knows that I am reading his mind and tells me . . . "Mom come to me." I follow the link, and Grady is right beside me. There are two more vamps they are all the way on the other side of the city. These two are not looking for food. It seems that they are having some sort of meeting. I read their minds, and they are discussing us. How they are not to attack us, that the Eleven need us alive now. How they wish they could be the ones to get the chance to kill us. I tell the boys what they are thinking.

"Well then we should give them that chance." Grady is smug when he says this. He knows that they are no match for the three of us. "Again Mom just stay back, and we will feed you." Grady moves around one side of the vamps and Jordan, around the other side. Before they could smell, or even sense them, my boys had both vamps by the necks, pressing them up against the wall.

"Well, I am guessing that you didn't think that you would really get the chance to kill us now did you?" Jordan asks the question knowing that these vamps have no idea who we are. "Oh, maybe you don't know who we are? Well, let me introduce us. We are the Dhampirs that you so very much wanted the chance to kill. I have to tell you, you aren't much of a fight for us. By the way, this is Mikatta Hope, and tonight she will be killing you." And with that I took the one that Jordan was holding. To say that my hunger was substantial was an understatement! By the time I was done with the second vamp, I did feel full finally!

"Let's get her home, I think that she should really save all her energy." Grady scoops me up and begins our run home.

"Ok that is it! You know I can do that myself put me down." I try to wiggle out of Grady's hands, but he is REALLY strong and I can't break free.

"No! Like I said you need to save your energy. The less you do the less you have to feed."

"Fine, but you know that I will get you for this somehow." Both Grady and Jordan laugh. They know that is a threat I will not make good on. I have way too much on my plate to worry about them trying to keep me safe for once. As we get closer to the ranch, the boys slow up a bit, they know I love the night air out here. Grady puts me down so I can walk the rest of the way home. They run up to the ranch. The air smells so pleasant, and the night is calm. I walk slowly to the ranch feeling full from the five vamps I have just finished off. I hear Dan coming to me his thoughts are of worry about me. He thinks that I am not doing well, that I am using all my strength to keep us safe. I am but I won't tell him that, no need to worry him anymore than needed.

"How are you my love? Did everything go well?"

"I thought the boys would have told you everything by now." I laugh a little as he wraps his arms around my waist and picks me up in his arms.

"I didn't wait to listen I needed to be with you."

"Yes it went fine. Although, I fed on one vamp, that was very old and I saw his maker. The last time I did that I ended up . . ."

"Killing Hanzi! Is that how he found you? By you killing one of the vamps he made?"

"Yes, but I don't think that it can be just any vamp, otherwise I would have seen all of them by now. It has to be an old vamp. I think they might be the first ones made from the originals."

"So what you are saying is that there are twelve of those that can link you to their makers. And when that happens that vamp can see you? They know what you have done?"

"I think so. I don't think that Persia feels the same about me as Hanzi did. He is the strongest strength wise of the Twelve. He is so strong that he could demo a building on his own. If he decides, to come after me, we could have some real trouble with him." I know that Grady is our strongest, but I don't know if he can take Persia. I will have to talk to Grady and see what we can do about boosting his strength just in case Persia comes for me. Dan carries me back to the ranch and puts me on our bed. Anthony runs and leaps on me with the tightest hug.

"I missed you Mommy! I am glad you are home."

"I missed you to sweetie. I am home, and I am not hungry anymore." I squeeze him back as I laugh.

"Mom, Dan said you might want to talk to me about something?" Grady walks into the room with a very concerned look on his face.

"Come sit next to us. And yes you all can hear this." I holler out to the other kids standing close by wanting to listen in. They are in the room in a blink of an eye. "Grady that one vamp the one that was fighting you, you had to hold on tighter to him because he was stronger than the other two. When I fed from him, I saw his maker." I tell them all what I have told Dan. This is a situation that we haven't come across before I don't know how we can beat this kind of strength. I know the only one that has any chance will be

Grady. I don't like the fact that my son will have to be the one facing Persia.

"Don't worry Mom, he isn't coming after us right this minute. We have plenty of time to prepare for him. We will practice you and Anthony giving me power boosts, see how long it holds up. Then with the rest of the family around I am sure that we will have no problem taking this Persia out." He looks at me with such confidence and strength. I know he truly believes that we can do this, and that nothing bad will happen to any of us. I still have that feeling, that it shouldn't be my son going up against this vampyer. For now I just want to rest a little, spend some alone time with my Husband.

We have gone out hunting every night. My hunger is very sizeable now that I am always using my energy. I am hoping that I will find a way to use less energy and still keep up our little mind block up. We have had to go to different cities. I can't believe how many of these lessers vamps, there are out there. I should be glad because I do need to feed off of them to keep my energy up. But still, I wonder if the Originals are still making these lessers? With the new mind block, I can't see these kinds of things anymore.

"Crysta, can you come here please?" I need her to look into the past see if she can see if they are making any more of the lesser vamps.

"Yea Mom what's up?"

"Sit I need you to look into the past, not the far past just like the last few years, see if you can see if the Twelve have still been making lesser vamps."

"Ok, I think that I can do that." She was quite for a few minutes. "Yes, and they have stopped being so picky about who they turn into vampyers anymore. Even now they are making them. I think they are even trying to double their numbers. It looks like they are worried?"

Crysta looks at me again.

"Yea I had a feeling that they were still making vamps. Although, I think that the reason that they are doing it now isn't the same reason as they were doing it before. I think that now the reason is to try and capture us. They know that we can take the lessers with no problem, so they need enough of them to capture us. I think we need to keep taking them out as fast as we can. It is a good thing that I am very hungry these days!" We laugh and have a quiet moment to ourselves. We talk about the time that she has been spending with Leham. I do think that she is letting her guard down with him just a little. She talks about him in a very soft and caring way. I don't need special gifts to know that she is falling in love with him. All of my Motherly instincts have kicked in as I tell her that it is ok to allow Leham into her heart, and that he isn't anything like her ex. It will take a lot of time and effort from Leham to break through all the walls that my daughter has built up. But I have seen what Leham feels for Crysta, he will break through them with all the love that he has for her. Crysta hugs me and gets up and leaves the room, and Anthony follows his sister out the door. I lay back and close my eyes I try to think of all the good that we have in this family.

"Mom, are you resting?" Kara's sweet voice comes through the door.

"I am dear, but you are always welcome to come to me with your worries." I can feel her heart hurting.

"I am so sorry to bother you. I just don't think anyone else would understand what I am feeling right now. Grady, he seems to just be playing around with me. I am not getting the feeling that he really loves me. Or even that he has any true feelings for me. You are the only one that knows him to the deepest parts. I know, I shouldn't ask you this question, but does he have any real feelings for me?" Kara has tears in her eyes, and I can feel all the pain that her heart is feeling. I do know what my son feels for this young woman, but I will not be the one to tell her his feelings.

"Kara, I love you sweetheart. But I cannot be the one to tell you what his heart feels. I know you are afraid to talk to him about his feelings. You have to go to him and tell him what you are feeling. This is something that you have to do with him. You can't be scared of what he will say. Because no matter what is said you are and always will be a part of this family, and that is not my way of saying anything. Kara, dear go to him and talk to him right now. You have to ask this question to him!" With tears in her eyes, she nods her head and leaves my room. I wanted to tell her what Grady feels for her, but if their relationship is going to work at all, they have to talk.

Tonight, we go out as a full family to feed. We are having to go further away from home each time we go out. I worry that we will, in one of our outings, end up meeting up with Persia. I don't believe that we are ready for him just yet. Grady is showing much more strength, and his fighting abilities are improving quickly. I still worry for my son. Jordan has found a large coven of vamps. He knows that I alone can feed on six of them. Jordan and Grady are guiding us to this new town, which seems like there are more vamps then humans. I have a really strange feeling about this trip. Anthony is on my back, so I can keep him safe, even though he looks like he is thirteen now. Dan is on my right side, and the girls and Leham are right behind us. Grady and Jordan come to a stop, so we can get beside them. Again, that feeling of something not being right hits me really hard, almost like I have walked into a brick wall.

"Wait! Something is not right here. I can feel something, I can't explain it. It just feels really wrong." I tell my family what I feel so that we can all know what is going on. "Grady what do you see inside?"

"Looks like about thirty of the vamps, some are feeding on humans others are just lying about. I can't see anything else that would look like we couldn't do this." Grady is sure of what he sees. I still don't feel right.

"Crysta, look into my future and tell me what you see." I know that we have to use all of our gifts to make sure that this is going to go the way it should. "And look into the close future, not the far future." She takes a minute to see my future.

"You seem fine Mom you are holding Anthony at home. But you said only to look into your future so I didn't see anyone other than you and him. Give me a minute to look into all our futures."

But she doesn't get that chance. Three vamps walk out the door and smell us and call the others. We have little time here to form our wall and take these vamps as food and not have to just kill them. In seconds, all of the vamps have formed a circle around us and are not attacking. They stand there as if they were told to wait. Then before I could tell my family what was coming Persia was right in front of me.

"Mikatta Hope! I have seen you, and you have taken my first from me. I will kill you here in this place."

I link my family together and tell them that Grady is to fight, and we are to be his strength. Dan pulls the shield from us, and we focus it on Grady. I push my energy into him. He starts to glow, and you can see that he is pulling in energy from around him. Kara does something I know is a bad move, but I can't stop her in time. She steps in front of Grady.

Persia sees her and takes one full hit to her chest, and she is thrown back about fifty feet. I feel her chest break! Grady is now angered and charges Persia. The two move so fast as they fight if you were a human you would only see a blur. But I see it all, I try not to go to my mother mode and be scared for him. Anthony takes my hand as he slides off my back, and he tells me . . .

"Let me project that feeling to him Mommy. It will help him." Anthony is right and he, and I link to Grady alone. I tell the rest of the family to begin to kill the lesser vamps and feed, we need more power. Dan, Crysta, Leeha, Jordan and Leham begin to easily take out the lesser vamps. Dan knows I need food and brings two of the vamps for me to feed on. I feel the power and give it to Anthony, so he can protect Grady. Persia is so strong, and I feel the hits that Grady is taking from him. They are all over the place. Then Grady sees that Kara is not moving at all. He turns to Persia and lands a hit right to Persia's face, and he goes flying into the building which is at least two hundred yards away from them at this point.

"Grady come here! Everyone come to me now!" I call to my family. We need to grab Kara and leave now that we have a chance. "Get Kara we are leaving now!"

Everyone moves like we are one entity, and we are gone from that place in seconds. Grady has Kara in his arms. I can read his fears. He didn't tell her that he really did love her last night when she came to him. Now he fears that she will die before he can tell her.

It takes us at least an hour to get clear of any of the vamps that were following, and we have put our mind blocks back up. In about half an hour we will be home. Grady lays Kara on the couch, and we all come to her side. I touch her chest and feel the damage that Persia has done to her heart. She has lost most of her own blood. I cut my wrist and hold it to her mouth. But she isn't drinking from me. I let the blood drip over the wound. But we all see there is nothing left of our dear Kara. Persia has killed her. Grady lets out the most heart-breaking scream.

"NOOOOOOOOOO Kara! You can't leave me, I didn't tell you the truth last night. Please Kara, don't leave me. I Love You! I do love you!" He grabs her and holds her close to him. He does not want to let her go. I feel the pain he has in him, and I try to touch his arm to help him feel less pain.

"No Mom, you can't take this away! This is my pain to bear leave me alone with her please?"

"Grady, we all loved her too. We all need to be able to say our own good-byes to her."

"Not now. I need to be with her. Please Mother give me this one thing that I ask." We know he needs this, and we all leave the room. I don't read my son's mind. I truly leave him there with Kara so that he may have his time. Anthony tugs on my hand.

"Mommy will you please hold me?" I pick up my youngest son and sit on the couch and hold him close to me.

Chapter Thirteen
Needing the Facts

We know now that we can die! Grady has been spending a lot of time alone. We buried Kara on the ranch, out back behind the house. There are these two giant old oak trees, and we laid her body to rest in between the trees. It was one of the saddest days since my Husband passed away. All of our hearts felt as if we had lost a part of us. Losing Kara like this was just too much of a slap to the face for our family. We had gotten very comfortable with the knowledge that we couldn't be touched by these vamps. I don't know what to say to my son. I know how I was when Kevin died. I felt as if there was nothing left for me to live for. If I didn't have my kids, I know I would have taken the easy way out. If my kids didn't come to live with me and force me to keep going I would have. I know I have to talk to him, to keep him focused on what we have to do. Instead of me talking to him Dan asks if he can. I felt that it wouldn't hurt for Grady to have a man to talk to. They went for a long walk in the woods, during the day just after breakfast. It was the most beautiful morning that I can remember.

"Grady, I want to tell you that I know what you're going through. However, I don't believe you would believe me. So I want to tell you what it was like for me when my wife just up and left me. I know it doesn't seem like that would be anything like you're losing Kara in the way you did, but I felt as if someone had taken a knife and just cut out half of me. I didn't know what I was supposed to do with the rest of my life. I didn't think that I wanted to go on, but Grady, you have a purpose! This family still needs you. I know that I am not your real father, and I would never try to take that place in your life. I do feel like you are my family, and I back my family up. I want you to know that I am here for you. I love you son!" Grady was silent for a little while, just walking with Dan.

"I lied to her the night before she died. She asked me if I was in love with her. I told her that I didn't know if I was there yet. That I enjoyed her and I wanted to keep getting to know each other, but that I didn't think I was in love with her yet. I had loved her from the moment I set eyes on her. I am going to KILL Persia! And not just for Kara, for this family. I have to tell you something that happened that night when we were running home. Kara wasn't dead when I got to her, she couldn't talk, but she was still conscious. As I was carrying her home, she gave all of her power to me. All the living energy that she should have saved for herself to stay alive she gave to me. She wanted me to have the extra boost so that I can kill him. And Dan, you are my second dad. I thank God that he gave us another chance on having a family. You make a really good Dad. Thank you for bringing me out here and talking to me. I really needed it."

Dan and Grady stop and there was that moment, then they gave each other a hug. This was truly something that I never thought that would ever happen again. I am sitting out front on the porch when suddenly I am hit with a vision of the past. Yes, I know Crysta gets the visions not me. So you can imagine my surprise when I see Crysta, Grady and I in the room with Justin and Nathan. Justin says . . .

"There are others like you and your children. Although I have to say, that you three seem to be the strongest of them all. I am proud to call you daughter." Then I was standing in a basement that was full of the blood packets and a computer that had names on it. I realized what I was being shown. These were the others that Justin had talked about. I was getting the feeling that we were to go there and see this. And to find these others that Justin had spoken of. We will need more like us if we are to stop the remaining Originals. When the vision is over, I see that I am lying on the porch and Grady, and Dan are trying to wake me.

"I am fine! I am fine! Just give me a second. I need to sit down for a minute."

"Mom it looked like you were looking right through us. Didn't you see us?"

"I said just give me a second. My head is splitting!" Dan opens his wrist and holds it to my mouth. I normally would have told him that I didn't' need it, but I really felt I should. I hold his wrist to my mouth and drink. Dan has the most amazing taste in his blood, and I don't want to stop. I push his arm away, and wipe my mouth. I then tell them of what I have seen. They both sit there looking at me.

"You think we need to go there and see what other names are on that computer don't you?" Dan asks with that, Oh goodness this is going to be rough voice.

"Yes I do. I get the feeling that I was shown that for a reason. And the way my head hurts after that, I don't want to go through that again if I can help it! Crysta can keep the visions." I laugh half-hearted and so does Dan and Grady. Crysta comes running out to the porch.

"Mom, are you ok? I think we need to get to that basement as soon as we can. We need those other Dhampirs to help us with all of this."

"Crysta Dawn Hope, did you send that vision to me?" I am not happy as I am asking this question.

"No Mom, I can't seem to share my visions with anyone just yet thank you very much. But I could tell that you were with me in the vision. I could feel you and your head hurting." Crysta sits next to me and holds my hand. I am feeling better now.

"So you both saw the vision?" Dan asks.

"I guess so. But I think Crysta might have gotten a much better view of where it is and maybe of how to get there?" I saw the lab just not how to get there. I know her visions are very clear, and they show everything to her.

"Yes, Mom I do know where it is, and how to get there. You need to rest, and we really need to get you some food. Hey, maybe the blood packets could help?" She asks this not just for me but for everyone.

"Well, I am guessing that it can't hurt, but let's get there and see what it is that we need to find there. Or should I say who we will find there." I don't want to rest. I just want to see what this vision was trying to tell me.

Everyone gets ready for our first outing without Kara. Anthony no longer needs to be carried to keep up with us. So we are all off trying to follow Crysta. We had to tell her to slow down more than twice. Man that girl has gotten even faster than she used to be. We get to Justin's and Nathan's house. She stops, and turns and looks at all of us and opens the door to the house.

"It has been here all along, just under the house and through a tunnel." We follow her through the house and down some stairs. There is a wall that seems that it is just a wall. But with our eyes we can see there is a door. We open it and enter a tunnel that looks like it might go on for miles. It only takes us a few minutes to reach the lab. It is a very sizeable lab with different types of equipment I have never seen before. And at least twenty large coolers that I knew were full of the blood packets. Grady and Jordan go to the computer to start pulling up all the work that Justin had done. They find the list of all the names of humans that had begun to go through the change. The amount of humans that had started the change was amazing.

"I can't believe how many people have started the change. What if they didn't get the chance to finish the change?" Jordan is worried that they may have been killed by the partial change. "Can you print off all the names and addresses for us? That way, we can try to find all these people and find out for ourselves, what has become of them." I ask Jordan.

"Of course I can. This place is set up for just about anything that we might need to find of whatever we want. The list is really long though. Are you sure we can take the time to find them all?" Jordan and Grady have the same thought about us changing what our plans are. That it might hurt us, by allowing the Originals to make more vamps.

"I think that we are going to need more help. As we have seen, we can be killed just like them." I say this is in a soft voice so that it doesn't hurt when I say it. Kara's death is still very raw for all of us.

"Mom, come see this." Leeha calls to me from the coolers. I walk up to see it full of the little packets that started this all. I reach in and take one packet out. I have no idea what drinking this will do to me, but my hunger grows, and I can't wait. I bite the side of the packet and drink it all. There is the blood of vampyers in these packets, and I want more. I drink until the hunger is gone, as does the rest of the family. All but Anthony, the packets do nothing for his hunger. He was not turned into one of us. He was born one of us. He can only truly feed by eating a real vampyer. Leham and I give Anthony some of our blood to drink for now. It doesn't fill him, but it helps more than the packets do.

"I think that we should take some of these packets with us. It might make it easier for the others to understand that we know what they are going through." Leham is right we are going to need an easy way of approaching this with these other people. If they haven't been fully changed than these might help us to prove to them that we know what they are going through. And that we can help them through this, if they will let us. We find some backpacks and fill them with the packets, partially for the ones, and partially for us. Just in case we don't find any vampyers along our way. This way, we can still feed on something.

The first person isn't that far from us, about thirty miles or so. It only takes us a few minutes to get there. We have decided that only two of us will go to the door. Seeing all of us at once might scare this person away. Carrie Keller is the first name on the list. The computer printed out that she is twenty-two years old, and that she took to the packets very well. Her change began after about a month. Grady rings the door bell, and he and I wait for her to answer. The door opens, and there standing in front of us is a very beautiful young woman who stands about five foot seven inches and looks as, if she should be on the cover of a magazine. Grady is mesmerized by this young lady and can't seem to speak.

"We are sorry to bother you miss. But we are looking for a Carrie Keller?"

"I am Carrie, and who are you?" She stares right into my eyes. She can see into my mind almost the same way I can read hers.

"Oh my God! Please tell me that you are real? I have been thinking that I was the only one that had gone through this weird thing." Carrie is very much excited to see us.

"May we come in? It would be better to talk about this inside. Don't you agree?" Grady still has no words to use, just stares like an idiot at Carrie.

"Of course come in. All of you she hollers out to the rest of our family. She could see them through my mind. Carrie was very excited to see that there were so many of us. But when she saw Anthony, she almost freaked.

"Oh no, don't tell me that, that, stuff changed a teenager?"

"No dear this is Dan and mine's son Anthony. He was born after we were changed."

"So what is he then? And for that matter what are we?" Carrie has truly been alone through this whole change. So we give her all the details of what we have learned. We tell her about our little and big battles with the vampyers. We tell her everything that she should know.

"How have you managed this long without killing a vampyer?" I have to know what has kept her hunger at bay.

"Well I sort of stocked piled those blood packets and have just been drinking off of those for now. It helps but I never really feel full." I feel her hunger, and want to get her a real meal.

"Jordan, can you tell if we have any vamps close by? I think we need to try and feed again."

"Sure Mom I can see if I can sniff some out. But you know that it will still have to be a lot of them. You can feed off of at least six of them." Jordan makes that sarcastic voice of a son to a Mom.

"Ha, ha very funny Jordan. Just see what you can find please?" I would slap him, but it wouldn't hurt. Of course, Jordan finds us the vamps we need. They are not as close as I would have liked. But we need to feed, and so did Carrie. It seems that there are plenty of vamps to go around, but I don't go into this without spending the time to read into their minds. They are all simple vamps. I do not sense Persia at all. Tonight should go very easy, but I still can't get the feeling of our last time we came up against vamps. Grady and Dan stand in front. The vamps are inside a community center. It seems they have made it their home. It looks run down and doesn't seem to have any electricity. I see flickering lights, candle light is enough for them to see very well. There are two ways in, we break into two groups. Dan heads up one group and Grady the other. We burst into the center at the same time from both sides. Crysta's voice begins it's song, and the vamps seemed stunned. Grady and Dan hit three each and knock them right to the floor. Jordan and Leeha group four of them together, they hold one vamp in one hand as they drink from the other. Carrie stands next to me and Anthony. She is unsure of what to do.

"It's ok Carrie the first time was strange for me to. But Mom will help you through it." Anthony goes for a younger girl that is trying to get around Grady and Dan. With ease my youngest grabs her arm, spins her around and bites into her neck drinking her blood.

I take Carrie's hand in mine, and I move us around Crysta and Leham, who have four of their own vamps to feed from. There are still eight vamps cornered in the center. They know that they can't get around us, so they decided that they will fight us two little girls. I let go of Carries hand, and I build a small amount of energy inside and push it out so I can hold it in front of the vamps.

"What the hell is that?" One of the male vamps asks.

"Well let me show you dear." I send the small amount of energy and spread it out to hit all eight vamps. It knocks them all to the ground and unconscious. I take Carries hand and lead her to the first male in the row. I kneel her down next to the vamp and cut a deep gash in his neck. Carrie smells the blood and cannot fight the hunger. She bites into his neck and feeds for the very first time. I move to the second in line, and drain her, then move to the third. Carrie is done with her first vamp and is at my side.

"Would it be alright if I had another?" She asks with a childish smile on her face.

"Yes Carrie dear, please have another." She takes the fourth vamp in line a girl and bites into her neck and begins to drink. I feed off of the remaining vamps before she finishes with her second.

"Is everyone ok?" I am asking in my mind and with my voice.

"YES" I hear all of my family's reply. Carrie calls . . .

"I can't believe how full I feel! Those packets really just don't have anything on the real thing, do they?"

We all laugh at the same time as we see Carrie and the mess she has made of herself. The blood covered more than half of her body. And she stood there with the most wonderful grin on her face. We make it back to Carrie's house, and everyone gets cleaned up. It takes Carrie longer but she does finally come out of her room.

"Carrie, we would like to ask you to come live with us on our ranch. It is quite far from here, but you would be with family?" Crysta asks Carrie what we all are thinking.

"I was so hoping you would ask me to come and stay with you. I have felt so alone for the past few months. Hell Yea, I would love to come!" She is so very happy that she seems to be glowing. I am not the only one to notice this.

Chapter Fourteen
Adding to the Family

Carrie fits right in with the family right now. She is so happy to have us. Turns out, she was living on her own because she lost her parents. They had passed away last year during a drunk-driving accident. She used to do some modeling, but when she lost her parents, she spiraled right downhill. She wanted something that would help bring her back from the hell, she had found herself in. She tried to work out again but found she just didn't have the energy. She tried drinking other energy drinks. But found that most made her sick to her stomach. She was looking at some clothes that she was thinking about trying when she saw the blood packets. Just like us, she began to drink them, finding as did we, that they gave her just what she was looking for. When the change came to Carrie, she was alone and had no Dhampirs with her to help with the pain that the change brings. As she told us, she has just been drinking the blood packets, until now. You could see it in her eyes the color was getting deeper, and her face was getting some real color. The sun does her good as we have our next outing to find the next Dhampir. The name on the list was Trent Tessitor. He was twenty-six years old and lived another thirty miles from Carrie's home. Again as with Carrie, we know it will be best to only have two of us come to the door to begin with.

This time Dan is with me, he knocks on the door, and we wait. It takes a few minutes, and then we hear . . .

"Come in." The man's voice is deep and doesn't sound as if he is running on all cylinders.

Dan and I enter the house slowly, listening to hear something that might be waiting for us. The smell hits us first, almost like rotting flesh. If it was, we knew what we were going to have to do. I link myself to the family, even Carrie is now in my link. We walk into the living room and there is no one there. So I call out to the young man.

"We are not here to hurt you. We believe that you are like us, and we can help you through all of this if you will come out and let us!"

"I DON"T WANT OR NEED YOUR HELP YOU FEEBLE HUMAN! I HAVE NO PROBLEM TAKING CARE OF MYSELF NOW! HAHAHA!" This is where, I know that the change has not gone the right way with this one, and call my family to me. Dan and I can tell that the young man thinks that he can take us, he only smells the human on us, not the Dhampir in us.

The family is now right at our back, as the young man Trent steps into the room with us. He is about five foot and eleven inches, not to tall, bright burgundy eyes and sort of dirty blonde hair. He stands there just looking over us, thinking that it doesn't matter how many humans that we are that it will never be enough anymore.

"Trent I am not a human, if you try you can smell that there is something else about us that isn't all human. You drank the same blood packets that all of us have, didn't you?"

"What difference does that make? I am so strong that none of you could even lay a finger on me. I have become much more than you will ever become."

"I am only going to tell you this once Trent, this is my family and there is nothing human or vampyer that I will ever allow to hurt them again. You are truly nothing to me Trent, but I do not wish to kill you if we can help you." I try to show Trent the power in my voice.

Trent did not respond with anymore words. He came at me with everything that he could gather. I shoved him to the side with only one of my hands, as the rest of the family stood still and watched. Trent gets to his feet and you can see the anger in his eyes now. Again, he tries to run at me with all his force, and again, I shove him to the side. He falls to the ground like a pile of dirty clothes. I turn to look him straight in the eyes to speak to him.

"The next time you come at me to harm me Trent, I will have no other choice but to kill you. And so that I am clear about what I am saying to you, that means my entire family as well." All of the power I can show him is in my voice now.

"What are you? How can you just shove me to the side without even trying? I know what power that I have, I have killed with it!"

"Who have you killed Trent? Have you killed humans?" I know what his answer is, and I know that I will not let this creature live!

"Yes I have. MANY OF THEM!" These are the last words, I let pass through Trent's mouth. In a blink, I am in front of him with his neck in my hand, holding him above me.

"I am sorry to say that this is our hello and goodbye."
I turn his neck quickly to the side, and Trent's body goes
limp. This is not what I wanted to have happen today. But
when we started this, we all knew that there was a small
chance, that we would find some of us that didn't make it
through the change. I was hoping that it wouldn't be so soon
though, but then again I didn't make all of this happen. I
was just here to kill the Vampyers!

We decided that we should only try one more for
today. Depending on which was closer. We could go back
to Carrie's or back to the Ranch. Andrew Linqust was the
next name on the list. To my happiness, Andrew lived pretty
close to the Ranch. I have to say I wanted to be at home for
a day or so. To learn more about our new members slowly,
and to take a nice hot bubble bath.

This time I have Crysta with me. She and I walk up to
the door and knock. I hear someone moving around in the
apartment. I link to Grady and tell him to see who is inside.
He lets me know it is just Andrew, but he stands a good
Six foot three inches. He asks me if Crysta and I will need
any of the men around for this one. Crysta sends back a
painfully sharp NO!

"Andrew, my name is Mikatta Hope. I know you have
been through a lot, and that you are really scared right now.
You see, my family and I, well you are just like us. If you
try, I bet you can tell that we are telling you the truth?" I
asked it almost as a question. Not sure yet if Andrew is like
Trent.

"What do you think that I am? Because to tell you the truth I have no idea what has happened to me in the past few months. I know I have felt the most horrible pain, and then now I feel no pain. Why is that?" He almost sounds like he is a child with the way he asks his question to me.

"Andrew, could you please let us in? It would be much easier for my daughter and me to talk to you if we were not yelling through a door?" I am hoping that he can tell that we will not hurt him. Then, the door opens and as Crysta and I look up there stands this extremely tall young name with dark-brown eyes and dark-brown hair.

"You can come in. Even the ones that are hiding from me, I can smell all of you. You all need a bath!" Andrew knows about the others, I just can't tell how yet.

We all enter into Andrew's apartment. It is small, and we sort of have to squeeze in order to fit. Andrew stands in front of us all and stares for just a moment, looking us over one by one. I was about to say something when Andrew starts in.

"We are all alike aren't we?" This is his first question to us.

"Yes we all drank from the blood packets, and we have all been changed by them." I answer him only because I get the feeling he hasn't had a mother for a very long time. He acts as if he would like to have me as one though.

"You all have different gifts from each other Mother, and Daughter share a similar gift. It is not quit the same gift. You have all killed vampyers too, haven't you?" This is Andrew's second question that he has for us.

"We have killed many of the lesser vampyers. They seem to be a source of food to us. And Mikatta here has killed one of the original Twelve vampyers all by herself." Dan says with all the pride that he can muster.

"I remember getting a little help from someone there husband dear." I smile and wink at my loving husband. Through all this I am trying to remember that we are still newlyweds and that, we really haven't had a lot of time to spend on that part of us.

"So you have come here looking for those of us that are like you. So that we can help you kill these vampyers?" This is the third question that Andrew has for us.

"Well, yes we have. The last Original vampyer that we went up against has the most amazing strength that we have seen yet." I pause only for a moment to think out my words. "We battled with him almost three weeks ago. His power is so great that we lost one of our family members to him. So we believe that it will take a few more of us to do any real damage to this one vampyer." I am holding back tears, as is most of my family. The thought of Kara's death still pains all of us and we have to hide that for now.

"We were wondering if you would like to come with us Andrew. We are Dhampirs, and as you know, we have gifts that we can use to take out these horrible vampyers. I know you would make a wonderful addition to our family." I say these words just like any other mother would talk to their kids, trying to talk them into that big play they are scared of doing.

"I will come with you all. Grady and I will stop this Persia, and not let Kara's Death go unpunished." Everyone gasped!

"Andrew, how do you know all of this about us? We told you little pieces but not the whole story?" Leeha speaks before the rest of us can find our voices.

"Oh, well I hear a voice he tells me things that are going on around me. Sometimes I don't hear the voice for days then in the past three days the voice has been telling me about you all coming here to take me with you. So I can know things that can help me when I need it most. Plus, I am almost as strong as Grady there. The two of us can take Persia. I want to help you all." Andrew leaves the room, when he returns, he has his bags packed and says to us . . . "If we start now we can be at the ranch in about two hours."

"Ok then, Andrew I am glad that you have decided to come with us dear. I believe that you were meant to be with our family." I truly meant it. There is something in Andrew's heart that is right. I am not sure how to explain it, when he talks, you can hear this little something. Like I said I don't really know how to explain it just yet.

Just, the pure thought of being able to go home energizes me. I am almost keeping up with Crysta for the first time in weeks. Anthony is pretty fast himself, running next to me. Carrie is next to Anthony. She tries to hide what she is feeling for my youngest son. She knows he is not what he seems. All of my children are getting happy as they see the Ranch, in the distance.

Crysta comes to a dead stop. I smell it to. It is another bad Dhampir. Grady and Dan run in front of me. They have the feeling that this Dhampir might want to hurt me for some reason. Andrew is in front of them in a flash.

"Please let me take care of the bad one. I have done it many times already. I know how to make it quick." Andrew has compassion for these creatures. I feel it in his heart. He feels as if they were not completed right.

"Are you sure that is what you want to do Andrew? I can kill it as well. My energy can hold it long enough then I can kill it."

"No I will do this to show you I can help." I feel the strangest sickness in my stomach, almost like I might throw up. Before I can even think, I feel a stabbing pain run right through my stomach. I look down, and a sword has been run though me. I pull away from the sword and jump behind Dan and Grady. Every one of my family has formed a circle around me, and Anthony is in the middle holding my hand sending me a little energy to heal me. I link us all together, telling Dan we could really use his shield right about now. Dan puts it up and Leeha stretches it around us and I try to find the Dhampir that has done this to me. It isn't me who finds him, it is Andrew.

"You hurt my new Mom! I was going to be nice to you, but now I just want you dead!" And just like that the Dhampir falls to the ground on his knees. Then Andrew walks to the bad Dhampir and looks down at him.

"Andrew wait, I want to know why he wanted to hurt me before you kill him." I come out of our circle, with everyone right behind me. I am standing in front of this thing looking down at it. It isn't a man. It is a pregnant female. I kneel down and take her hand.

"I didn't change right! I wasn't pregnant when I started the change." The only thing holding her where she was, is Andrew's will. "I got pregnant in the middle, when it started to go wrong. I know I can't have this thing be born. I saw you kill his Daddy, and I was hoping you would kill me to. I don't know what this is inside of me. But you can't let it be . . . AAAHHHHH!" She lets out a horrifying scream her body is thrown back against the ground.

"Andrew, No wait!"

"Momma it isn't me it is the baby!" She is still screaming and her body is being rolled around, then I feel it, just like when she stabbed me with the sword. Her belly opens up. We are all to close, and her blood is now all over us. The sound is not that of a new-born baby. It hurts our ears as we look down to see this horrifying creature. It has fangs and claws, and its eyes are pure red. I know what must be done and build up all the energy that I can inside. I pull from everyone around me. With a tear in my eye, I send the energy right to the creature. Just like the lesser vamps the creature is turned to dust. I fall to my knees and for the first time I sleep.

Chapter Fifteen
Home Again

Darkness isn't always welcoming, but sometimes it is needed. I can feel my body and know that I am still with it. I feel as if I am detached from it in some form. Then suddenly there is light, bright and warmth. I could feel warmth all around me, wrapping me like a thick soft blanket. Then I could see a form in front of me no face just a form glowing almost a gold color.

"You are doing my work. You are what you are because of me. Evil has taken too much. I need you to stop them. They are stronger than you right now, and they are finding ways to become even stronger. They want to use you, and the family that I have given you. I know that you have the power within you, because I have given it to you to stop them. Your children, all of them will find you. I am sending them to you. When they get to you, I will tell you what I need you to do. I know you have questions, and I will answer them all in time. Your family is worried and they need you back. Mikatta, I chose you for this, not Nathan and Justin. Yes the packets are what caused the change in you but your gifts and everything that keeps you from being evil like them. I did. There are more of the damaged ones. They will have to be destroyed. Remember that I love you and your family and I will watch over you. And yes I had to take Kara from you. Grady needs to embrace his power and has not done that yet. He will now, and the next time you all meet with Persia the outcome will be better." Before I could ask anything or say anything I felt my body reconnect and I could hear my family.

"Mom, please wake up! Please don't die we can't do this without you." Crysta was sobbing and holding my hand.

"Stop it Crysta she can't die you know that!" Grady's tone is angry, but scared too.

"Both of you stop I am fine." Everyone makes some sort of sound of happiness. Dan scoops me up in his arms and holds on tight, and whispers in my ear so only I can hear.

"Please, I beg you to never do that to me again my love. I can't live without you. I won't live without you." I feel a tear on my neck. His love for me is so filling I wrap my arms around him and tell him . . .

"I will never leave you my dear. I love you too much to leave you ever." I pull myself back and sit up. "Something very strange just happened to me. I saw someone, the one that created us. He told me a lot of information, and I need to tell you all what was said. So, everyone sit down and just listen to me and there are no questions to be asked. Because I didn't get to ask any." I sort of laugh then I tell them what I was told.

"So we don't have to go out looking for the rest of the ones on this list?" Jordan sounds very relieved.

"No, they are coming to us now. I know that it all sounds sort of bizarre, but I know that everything happens for a reason. We are here to stop these vampyers. Together we can do it, even with all the power that they have. They are missing something that we have along with our power!"

"What is that Mom?" Leham asks.

"We have each other. We have our love for each other. They don't have that same love. Our love and the fact that we are family gives us way more power than they could ever have. Love is the most powerful gift, we could have ever been given." I look at Grady as I say this because I know his heart is angry because his love was taken from him. "Grady son, come sit with me, I need to talk to you alone." Everyone gets up and leaves the room.

"I don't want to hear how this was for the best, me losing Kara." He is very angry.

"I know son, I can't say that I blame you for what you feel. Your gift of strength is something that we need right now. You had not fully embraced it until that day. You sent Persia flying son. You embraced the gift that you had. All you wanted to do was kill him. Loss is something that you and I know already, and we both know that sometimes we have to lose something to gain what we really need." Grady takes my hand and looks me in the eyes.

"I know Mom. You lost Dad, and we thought we might almost have lost you then. Remember how you didn't want to live anymore without him? But Crysta and I made sure that you got out and lived. You have been doing the same for me. I know that I didn't tell her I loved her, but I did Mom, I truly loved Kara." He hangs his head, and for the first time since her death, Grady cries. I hug him tight while he cries away his loss.

"And now I have Dan. You will find someone else someday as well son. I have to tell you something else, if for no other reason than to hopefully stop you from getting hurt." Grady looks at me with that, ok Mom now, what are you talking about, look. "Carrie has very strong feelings for Anthony."

"Mom, I know that I was speechless when we met her, but that was only because she is like DUH beautiful. I don't have any other feelings for her. I promise! You are right I will find someone someday. Thank you for being my Mom, I love you!" And with that my oldest son gets up and leaves the room. In the next couple of weeks Dhampirs begin to show up at the ranch. The first one was a young man named Jacob Stallen. He is twenty nine-years old light, brown curly hair and green eyes. He was a doctor when he started drinking the packets, he thought it was just another one of those fad energy things. When the change hit him, he knew that he had to find anyone else that this might have happened too. The next and only other one to arrive is Dawn Haven. She is thirty-four years old. Single with no kids, she never felt like she was comfortable around other people. She has dishwater blonde hair and brown eyes. I think she reminds me of what my sister would have looked like if she would have lived. My sister was only a baby when she died of SIDS. Dawn was quite when she showed up. She didn't really want to tell us too much about herself, but after a day with me, she was ready to spill the beans.

Again, I am beginning to feel the hunger, as are the rest of the family. The only problem is now we are too many to go out at once. So we decide that it would be easier if we split into two groups. That way, we could look for smaller groups of vampyers, and then there would be less chance of us running into one of the Originals.

Anthony is beginning to have some real feelings for Carrie. And she is having those same feelings for him. They have spent a lot of time together over the past two weeks. I tell Dan that I think it is time for us to have "The Talk" with, both of them. We are not normal humans, and if they were to get pregnant, well it would really make things difficult right now.

"First of all we have noticed that they two of you have been spending a lot of time together. And no, we do not think that it is a bad thing. But being what we are you both need to know about what it is like having a Dhampir baby." Before I could finish Anthony speaks up.

"Mom I know exactly what it is like. I remember being born it was the first time you and I linked. You were telling me that the way I was coming was wrong. So you told me the right way to be born. So, you don't have to go through all of this with us."

"Son, we are not talking to you about this because we want you to know about the birth of the baby, but because of how difficult it would be if you two were to have a baby right now. Before you can become a Dad, I would like it if you became a husband. And to tell you the truth, I believe, you're too young for both." Dan steps in with his fatherly advice.

"Mr. Edwards, I don't want to have a baby just yet. I know that it is a very painful event even as a normal human. From what Anthony has told me, if Mikatta, here couldn't link to him to tell him what he needed to do he would have torn his way out of her. Now that is really not something I want to experience anytime soon. I also want to be married before I become a mother. I understand how old Anthony truly is. And it is not three months old. His heart, soul, and mind are the same age as anyone of us." She speaks with her heart.

"I know my son is not a child. I have watched him grow, be it very fast. He is still my baby, and there is much, he still has to learn before he can become a husband and a Dad. I love you both and only want your lives to be wonderful together. If that is what you chose to do. Right now we are not in a position for any of us to be having a baby. Now that we know how quickly our babies grow." I can't go through another loss of one of my family right now.

"We understand Mom. We promise that nothing is going to go on between us that shouldn't at our stage in our relationship. We know the road ahead of us isn't an easy one. We wouldn't want to put our own child in any danger as well." Anthony stands up walks over and kneels down in front of me and takes my hands. "I love you Mom and I will never do anything that will hurt you in anyway. Carrie and me will not give you any reason to worry we swear this to you." Anthony lays his head in my lap. I brush his thick blonde hair with my hand.

"Thank you son, I really did need to hear it from your lips."

Our newest members seem to be settling in very nicely. Everyone is getting to know each other, and learning our gifts. It turns out that Dawn has a gift for using the elements. She can control earth, wind, fire and water. Not on a big scale but enough to use as a distraction. Jacob is extremely smart. Smarter than I could ever think someone could be. It seems him being a doctor will help us even more now. His thought process is very fast, and he can think his way through things very easily.

Everyone has been practicing their gifts. Grady has been running little mock battles. All of this has made us all very hungry again. This means we must go out again in our little groups. Jordan is working overtime tracking down small groups of vamps for us. He has found three small groups for us to break up into and feed. We have stayed far away from where we had run into Persia. It has been a while, since we have split up and not taken the vamps out altogether. We feel this is safer for now. Unfortunately, all three groups are incredibly fair away from each other. So if something was to go wrong, we may not be able to make it to each other to help. So we have to be very careful, and take all the precautions to make sure that we lose no one. We break up into our groups Leeha, Jordan and Andrew are in one group. Crysta, Grady, Jacob and Leham are in group two. Then there is Dan, Anthony, Carrie, Dawn and myself.

We all leave at the same time in three different directions. Grady's group reaches their vamps first. There are a total of seven them, with Crysta singing the vamps are confused and aren't ready for Grady, Jacob and Leham to knock them all to the ground. Crysta grabs one vamp and with ease feeds. The boys make a game of it, which one of them can finish first. No hitches in their mission.

My group is the next to reach our vamps. We have around ten vamps, because I eat more than the others. Dan raises his shield and I begin to build up my energy. Anthony breaks my energy into ten little balls, and we push them into the vamps. This knocks all the vamps unconscious. This makes for easy feeding for all of us.

Leeha's group is the last to reach their vamps. They have seven vamps as well as Grady's did. Leeha starts to move the vamps all close together in a circle. Andrew takes a flying leap at them to knock them out. Before anyone could stop it, one of the vamps stabs Andrew with a knife. Leeha tosses the vamp as hard as she can against the wall. Jordan takes the others and pins them on the ground. Andrew rushes to the one who stabbed him and feeds off of him. The others get their fill as well.

Chapter Sixteen
The Time Has Come

"Holy shit!" I drop to my knees holding my side. Dan, Anthony and Carrie are at my side.

"Mikatta, what is wrong? Are you hurt?" Dan asks all the questions. When I pull my hands away from my side, there is blood on my hands. "What happened I didn't think you got hurt, let me see." Dan pulls up my shirt to find there is no wound. He looks again at my hands, and the blood is gone.

"Ok what is going on? I saw blood on your hands Mom, where did it go?" Anthony and Carrie both stand there just staring at me.

"We need to get to Andrew. He got stabbed during their feeding." We all rush back to the Ranch. When we get back to the ranch, Andrew has already healed and is bumping against chests with Grady showing their manhood. "Andrew, what happened to you?" I ask him all motherly like.

"Oh no big thing a vamp got lucky, that's all." Andrew laughs and shows us his side, which has healed up without a scare, much like when I was stabbed with the sword.

"Why in the hell did I feel that, and why did I see blood on my hands when I touched my side?" We are all still really new to this world, and we are all learning about what we are and can do together.

"You were staying linked with all of us weren't you?" Jacob asks me?

"Yes, I know I shouldn't have, but I can't just unlink from my family when we are apart like that. I need to know how everyone one is, or I just can't focus."

"Well that is probably why you felt what happened to Andrew. Your link is getting stronger with us now you can not only read our minds you can now feel how we are feeling. I believe that you could even completely connect with one of us."

"Jacob what on earth are you talking about? Completely connect with one of you? Do you mean that I could like blend with one of you and sort of be part of you?" The thought of me being able to combine myself with one of my family members is in one way, very interesting. Yet, in another way very scary.

"Yes I believe that you could do that. I think you are going to have to work on it a few times though. But it could possibly give us a new kind of power boost!" Jacob is very excited about the thought of this.

"I really don't like this having to split up while we are feeding. We need to find a way to not have to feed so much. Or find something similar to the packets that we can make stronger." I just can't take it anymore. I can't have us going out on these split hunting missions. The risk is so much greater than if we were together.

"I think that I have an idea about that Mikatta. Can you take me to the lab where all the packets were made?" Jacob being a doctor and all I should have known that he would want to see where all of us began this change.

"Yes we can. You think that there is something that you can do to help us not have to go out on these feedings?" I pray he can do something to help us with that. I sense something coming towards the ranch. I hear the thoughts of a young man. He is a Dhampir, but I sense something different about him. I don't believe he can tell that I am reading his mind. His thoughts are of confusion, he doesn't know if he likes what he has become. However, he is being called to this place. We meet him at the entrance to the ranch.

"Hello there, welcome to our Ranch. I am Mikatta this is my husband Dan and our family. And who might you be?"

"My name is Derek. I don't know if I want to be here. But something keeps calling me to this place. What are all of you?"

Derek makes me feel very uncomfortable. I can tell there is something wrong with him.

"Like you, we are all Dhampirs. You drank the blood energy drink and now you are half-vampyer and half-human. Have you feed yet?" Dan is sensing what I am feeling and he is stepping in front of me.

"I have feed. But it didn't fill me."

"What did you feed on Derek?" Dan is tensing and so is the rest of my family.

"A human, I craved blood, but it did not fill me. Why am I still so hungry?" Derek doesn't understand why we are acting so different now.

"Because you are not supposed to eat humans! You are supposed to eat vampyers. How could you have eaten a human? Why would you have done that?" Crysta asks all these questions, with pain in her voice. Grady is now in front of me as well. I have linked with everyone now. "Look, if you would like, we can help you with the change. We can even help you feed from a vampyer. It will fill you, and you will be able to rest from the hunger pain." Crysta is talking nicer now than when she first started, she is trying to calm Derek so that he will lower his guard to her.

"You can make this hunger go away?" Derek sounds surprised that we could help him.

"Yes, we are all here together because of the same reason. We want to help you. Derek I have to ask you this because you are like us, but may I look into your past?" Crysta doesn't want to wait, she sees something in the future that she doesn't like and wants to see his past.

"Why do you need to see into my past?" Derek sounds angered now.

"Please, do not think I am trying to hurt you. I have looked into everyone's past here. It only helps us to help you." Crysta is using a little of her voice to sooth Derek now.

"Fine, you may look into my past. I will tell you now, that you may not like all that you will see in there little girl!" Derek is being disrespectful to my daughter because he feels that we are disrespecting him.

Crysta closes hers eyes and begins to look into Derek's past. Tears form in my daughter's eyes and she begins to shake. Leham holds her firm in his arms. Crysta tears begin to turn to blood, and I come to my daughter holding her head in my hands looking into her mind. I see Derek changing into a Dhampir alone with no one to help him. The pain he is in. Then we flash to Derek killing the woman as he drinks her blood. We are taken further back, and we watch Derek beating up on a little kid about half his age, and I would say that he must have been around fifteen. He breaks the little boy's arm and bloodies the boy's eyes. I pull Crysta out of Derek's past and back into my arms. We are sitting on the ground holding each other. I look into my daughter's eyes, and the blood is gone.

"What the hell did they see Derek that would do that to them?"

Leham and Grady are in Derek's face as Leham asks the question.

"I told her she may not like what she sees in my past. I wasn't a very nice person. But I would like to change that and become part of your family if you will let me?" He sounds like he is speaking the truth, but I still have a very strange feeling from him.

"You may stay here tonight, and we will take you to feed. But hear my words very clearly Derek! One toe out of line and you will see just how powerful this family is. As of yet you are not part of this family and will have to prove that you belong with us." Dan is standing with Grady and Leham now, and the three of them take Derek to the Ranch. The rest of the family gather around Crysta and me and begin to ask their questions.

"What we saw was a young and very angry boy. Who has now turned into a very angry Dhampir!" I tell them after they have all asked the same thing. What did you see?

Only Dan, Grady, Andrew and Carrie go on the hunt for a vampyer for Derek. Carrie asks to come along because she believes that her mind reading might help incase Derek tries something. Anthony doesn't want her to go at all, but she tells him that he has to trust her, and they have to know that they can be apart. He reluctantly lets her go. Crysta and I look into their futures and see that they will return to the Ranch.

I decide that now is the perfect time to take Jacob to the lab so that he can start his work. This way if there is something not right with Derek, he won't know where the lab is, and we won't have to worry about Jacob's work not getting finished. The night is so clear, and the smells take me back to that warm feeling. I know that at some point our family will get the chance to live our lives without all this chaos. We get to the lab in no time, and Jacob seems like a kid in a candy store as he walks into the massive lab that was used to make the blood packets that changed us all. I can tell that Jacob missed being in that medical environment. Leham shows Jacob around and where all the files are in the computer so that he can get started right away. Crysta and I go back to the house. We both need to clear our heads of the visions that we saw, and I need to know what she saw before I linked with her.

"I don't think we should keep him here with us Mom. He has killed more than one human since his change. I could feel that he liked the kill."

"Maybe after he kills a vamp he will change what it is he likes to kill. My bigger fear is that I don't think he was meant to change into a Dhampir. In fact I don't think that he is a full one. He doesn't feel right to me. It feels a lot like Trent and his girlfriend. And we can't just let him run around killing people." We go through the house looking from room to room. Nathan and Justin had a very beautiful home. The bathroom is huge and has the most amazing bath tub. I feel so dirty and tell Crysta I just need to take a nice hot bath and get clean. She continues her search through the house as I start my bath. The bubbles smell like a wonderful lavender and feel like silk against my bare skin. I dunk my head under the water to get my hair wet and to get that wonderful smell into it. While I am under the water, I close my eyes, I have never been really good with keeping my eyes open under the water. There behind my closed eyes is the form that spoke to me before.

"You are on the right path my child. And you are right about Derek. You must watch him closely. Carrie is meant for Anthony, and you and Dan will have another child very soon. Jacob knows what it is that you need to survive without the vampyers. That way, you can kill them all, and still be able to live without their blood. Leeha will need your help with her baby. You will need to guide it into the world as you did Anthony. I know you have questions for me, but this is all you need for now. Keep Andrew close to you, you will need him soon."

I come out of the water quickly. Crysta is standing there with clothes in her hands.

"Look at this Mom. It looks like Justin and Nathan liked there women dressed nicely. Now you can put something clean on as well. Plus, I think I really could use a quick shower." And with that she was off to the shower. I sit there in the tub, not sure if I imagined what I saw, or if it was real.

I know what I felt was real, and that when I felt him the first time it felt right, just like this time. I take my time getting out of the tub and dressed. Crysta comes around the corner all clean and in new clothes.

"I fell so much better now, don't you Mom?"

"Yea, I feel way better. Let's go see how Jacob is doing. With his new speed, he should be able to find what we need a lot faster than when he was a human."

Back down in the lab I can hear the laughter and all the yelling, Crysta and I run into the lab to see what is going on.

"What is it everyone?" I ask.

"I got it! It was too easy though really. I have to give most of the credit to Justin. He left a lot of clues for me to pick up on. We are going to need to get some real vamps down here though. We are going to need a lot of real vamp blood to get me started."

"Oh sure, that will be a piece of cake! Jacob, how in the hell are we supposed to get live vamps all the way down here?" Jordan is the one to ask before the rest of us can.

"I never said I knew how to do that. I just said that we have to get them down here." Now that was going to be a little difficult. Us killing vamps has gotten harder. How are we to get live vamps all the way down here without anyone getting hurt? I know that we must figure out a way to do it. We can't live without the blood, and we can't leave, not even one of those things alive. Jacob gathers up a few things that he can take back to the Ranch with him. The smell of lavender is strong around me, and as we run home, I can smell it mix with the night air. We get back just before Dan and the rest.

"How was your trip?" I ask Dan.

"Derek has eaten." Dan gives me that read my mind look, so I read it and see that Derek liked killing the vamp, but not in the normal way. He tore the vamp up in pieces as he was drinking. I link to Grady.

"Son, you and Andrew stay with him. Do not let him out of your sight!" Grady nods in understanding.

"Do you fill full now Derek?" I ask very carefully.

"I do fill full now. Thank you for helping to find what my food source is." He speaks with no feeling what so ever.

"Well good, Grady and Andrew will show you where you can get cleaned up." I am still trying to talk as sweet and calm as I can.

"Ok, whatever." Grady and Andrew show Derek to the room where the three of them will share, so that the boys can keep their eyes on him.

"Dan, Jacob found what we need to make the blood. The only problem is that we will need to get live vamps all the way down into the lab. And keep them there alive." I tell my husband as we finally get some time alone in our room. "How do you feel about us having another child?" It just comes flying out of my mouth without me being able to stop it.

"Ok, wow first thing, I think we can manage the vamp thing, and second, I want to have many babies with you." Dan takes me in his arms and kisses me as he pulls me back onto the bed. I know what is going to happen, this baby is meant to be now. As the baby grows inside I call the kids to me so that this time, there won't be anyone worrying. I keep Grady and Andrew with Derek. I don't want him anywhere near my daughter. I know better this time what needs to happen, and my daughter is born with no pain at all. She has the most amazing smile, and of course, she has blonde hair. Her eyes are the same color as mine, purple. Crysta and Leeha just can't get enough of their little sister. Carrie comes up to her and steals her from the girls so that she can hold her.

"Hey, that is so not fair." Leeha calls out. She then runs to Carrie and the three just stand there staring at baby Kelana. They give their sister back to me as they get ready to go get the new girl baby clothes. We still have all the stuff that we got for Anthony five months ago, so we just need the basics. Dan slides next to me and has tears in his eyes. I hand him his daughter.

"My love why are you crying?"

"In the last five months I have been giving a wife and four children, and six added kids. I have to say I have a renewal on my life. I think we all got a renewal on our lives." Dan holds me and his daughter close. Anthony comes running into the room to see his little sister, with a huge smile on his face.

"Mom, she looks just like you and Crysta! Only she has your eye color. Can I hold her?"

"Of course you can don't be silly. Do you know what her name is?" I ask him this only to hear him say her name.

"Kelana is the best name you could have given her Mom."

"You should know better son. I didn't name her. She told me what her name is, just like you did." He has the biggest smile on his face. Kelana smiles back at him, then Anthony looks at me and starts to say something, but I stop him.

"Yes son I know she is hungry. Give her to me." Anthony hands me his little sister and sits next to me as I begin to feed her.

"She drinks your blood as well as the milk that your body gives her doesn't she?"

"Yes she does, but don't you remember that?"

"I do I just am thinking about when Carrie, and I have one and all of these things that she is going to have to go through. I want to remember everything so that I can help her with every part of it."

"I feel so strange that you are only five months old, and you are talking about having your own kids already. I almost feel as if you have been robbed of your childhood." Dan is still in awe of how our lives have moved so fast.

"No Dad I have gotten to be everything at just the right time for who I am. I am the son of the first great Dhampirs. My father is the most remarkable protector. And my Mother, well there just are not enough words to say how marvelous you are. You are the foundation of this family, and you are what makes this all feel so right." Tears come to my son's eyes.

"If you cry you will make me cry my sweet boy. Thank you for being such a wonderful son. I thank God that he gave you to me!"

"HA you think that God has done all this? Wow, maybe I have come to the wrong place after all." There in my doorway stands Derek with a look of hunger and hate on his face.

Chapter Seventeen
Evil Within

"If that is truly how you feel Derek feel free to leave. I don't believe that you want to be here anyway." I know I shouldn't tell him to go, but after hearing in his voice, the hunger that I think he might have for my daughter, I couldn't stop myself.

"Derek, we know you are not like us. We know that you have other ideas of how you want to live. And if you stay here you will give us the respect that you owe us for taking you in! Do you understand that?" Dan has gotten up from our bed and moved right in front of Derek.

"I got you big man, sorry I said anything. Cute kid and I just love the way you are feeding her. Looks like, she loves getting her drink from Mommy!" Derek is gone before I can say anything to him.

"Ok that is it. I can't take it! We really need to handle him. He is not the right kind of Dhampir and I don't want him around Kelana. I think he would kill her if he had the chance. I am not about to let that slimy piece of nothing hurt my family." I can't hold back the anger any more.

"Well, then I think we should take him out and leave him right near where we found Persia and let him take on those vamps. See if he can hold his own or not. We only found two vamps last night, and he didn't really do anything to fight them. We did all the work and all he did was made a mess of himself while ripping them apart." Dan knows Derek can't fight like we can.

"You know what I think you have an idea there. I want him to fight a vamp on his own. See if he has the power to kill one of them by himself. I don't believe that he is a full

Dhampir, and this will prove it. We need to get everyone together so that we can plan another hunt." I won't be going. I can't risk anything happening to Kelana. I know that she will need to feed a lot, and at some point I will feed again, but not while Derek is still around. She will not be out of my sight for even a moment.

Jordan has found a small-group of vamps that will not be anything for them to take out. And we tell Derek that they are going to feed again tonight, and he is welcome to come. He is very excited about it and is all in. Dan and the rest of the boys all go out with Derek to the vamps.

As they get closer Grady slaps Derek on the back and says . . .

"Why don't you go first buddy?"

"No that's ok I will just follow you guys." Derek's voice is not so tough anymore.

"No man, you will be going in first this evening. We need to be sure that you can handle your own if we get into a big fight you know?" Jordan adds in.

"I am still pretty new at all this you know. I think I should do more of the watch and learn thing. I mean at least until I understand how all of you work together." The fear is building in his voice, and he does not want to be the first in.

"Dude, either you go in there, or you're not eating tonight. We all have to pull our own weight around here. Man we will be right behind you." Jacob knows that Derek isn't going to go in alone so he gets up behind Derek. "Come on, it is a rite of passage." He yanks Derek up to his feet and gives him a nice shove. The rest of the boys follow them to the vamps. Derek is shaking noticeably, and all the guys know that he just might not make it out of here tonight. They are not going to help him with the vamp that he chooses. They get right up on the vamps, and Derek tries to take the small one. The guys take on the rest with no problems, but Derek is not having such luck. He doesn't have the strength to take a vamp by himself. Dan and the boys have already killed their vamps and they watch Derek struggle with the little one he picked. They want to help him, but I have given strict orders that if he is to stay, he must do this on his own. The vamp takes a good bite out of Derek, and he lets out a horrible scream. Leham takes a step forward to help, but Grady holds him back.

"You know that Mom wants him to do this by himself if he is to stay." Leham nods his head and steps back. Derek is trying everything that he can but this vamp is too powerful for him and he knows that this is going to be his end.

"Please help me!" He calls to my family. No one replies to him. Derek is now feeling the pain that he caused the humans that he has killed. I have been watching from inside his mind, and I talk to him.

"You are not right Derek, and now you feel the pain that you have given to the humans that you killed. You can never be part of our world. I am not going to allow you to live any longer. I cannot allow you to cause any more pain to anyone else. I was told that you were to die Derek, and now you will." I break the link as the vampyer sucks the last blood from Derek, and his heart stops beating. The vamp no sooner kills Derek then my husband is at the vampyer and holding it above the ground.

"My wife is hungry and you are going to be her dinner." The boys all grab a limb and rush the vamp back to me. Leaving Derek there with the rest of the dead garbage. I meet the guys outside the Ranch, and I am so hungry that I waste no time drinking the vamp dry.

"I am sorry that I asked you to do that. I knew that there was something not right with him. There are more of them like Derek out there, and we will have to take care of them as well."

"Great, because having the lesser vamps, and the Originals, to deal with isn't enough for us to do?" Jordan is almost throwing a fit like a little child at this point.

"Oh stop, why don't you use that energy and get rid of this dead thing?" Grady tosses the dead vamp to Jordan. Jordan takes off running with the vamp thrown over his shoulder.

"Ok now that we have taken care of that little evil, there is a wonderful baby girl who just can't wait to have her family back home with her. So let's go have some down time." I race them all back to the Ranch where Carrie is holding Kelana with her little arms out stretched to her Daddy. Dan scoops up his baby girl and holds on tight to her. Suddenly, both Dan and Kelana begin to float above the ground.

"Dan she can levitate. She has you both above the ground. I wonder if that is the only gift that she has." I pull Dan and Kelana back to the ground and take her out of his hands. I hold Kelana close to my chest, and I look into her mind. She knows I am there and is happy. Inside her head, she speaks to me.

"Hi Mommy, I have your gift as well. Not as strong and it is only electricity. I can make it come out of my hands." I see her smile, and I leave her mind.

"Well don't make her mad." I laugh. "She has quite a shocking personality. She can make electricity come out of her hands as well." I am happy that my daughter can talk to me just like Anthony did. I like knowing what they are thinking at that baby age, because with my kids, it doesn't last long. In five months, she will look as if she is twenty-two years old. Tonight, we all just hang out and spend some of the first family time together in a long time. Dawn comes over to me and sits down.

"I want to show you how my gifts work. Would that be ok with you?" She is so shy, and I am happy she wants to show me her gifts.

"I would honored if you showed me your gifts. Would it be safe for me to bring Kelana? I think she would like to see them as well."

"I would love it if she came as well." Dawn has a smile on her face. That is something that I have never seen on her before, she has a wonderful smile. We go out to the back of the Ranch house, just off the back porch. She steps a little ahead of us and raises her hands. All of a sudden a very soft gentle breeze begins to play around Kelana and me. It blows through our hair and tickles our necks, we both let out a little laugh. Then Dawn lowers her hands beside her and only moves her fingers. I can feel the ground below me rumble as if it wanted to lift me right up in the air. The rumbling stops and her eyes open, there is a well not far from where we are standing, and she looks at it. Her eyes turn pure blue. The water rises from the well and flows like a river right towards Kelana and me. It stops just in front of us Kelana reaches out her tiny hand and touches the water. She smiles and in our special way of talking to each other, she tells me . . .

"Momma it is cold." Then she laughs.

"I can't make fire. I can control it if there were some." With that Kelana reaches out her hand and sends just a little electricity out of her finger to a bush not far from us. "Why thank you Kelana." Dawn moves her hand, and the fire follows her movements. Then she uses the water to put the fire out.

"Dawn that is incredible that will so come in handy when we really have to fight the vamps. They won't know what hit them. I am truly glad that you have joined us Dawn." She and I laugh. I think this is the first time that I have seen Dawn happy, since she has come to us.

"Hey what are you three doing out here?" Andrew is standing on the porch with the rest of the family now.

"Sorry, Dawn was just showing us her gifts. She is really going to come in handy, let me tell you." I put my arm around her, and I pull her close to me as I smile at our family.

"Mom, you need to get in here right now!" Jordan is screaming at me from their room. I am up and in the room in seconds. There on the bed is Leeha getting ready to have a baby rip its way out of her pregnant belly. I kneel at the bed and put my hands on her stomach. I link myself to the child within her.

"There is a better and easier way for you to be born sweet child. I know you are scared, but you will really hurt your mommy if you come out this way." I tell the baby the right way to be born, and in only minutes Leeha is holding her baby son Kyle. Jordan has the biggest smile on his proud Daddy face, as he takes the baby from Leeha, so the girls can clean him up and get him dressed with Anthony's old baby clothes.

"Ok you two, why didn't you tell me that you had decided on now to start your family?" I ask in the nicest Mommy way that I can without sounding mad.

"We are sorry Mom. But you didn't tell us that you were going to have Kelana now did you?" Leeha has that sweet little smile on her face, that as a Mom you just can't be mad at.

"No But you must have been in some real pain there for a little bit?" I ask her.

"I was, but I wanted to be able to feel some of the pain of having a child. I will never get to know what it was like to have a baby the way that you had Crysta and Grady. So I wanted to be able to feel something." I could understand exactly what she was saying. I loved being pregnant with my kids and going through the labor and birth were all very beautiful.

"Ok but next time would you please let me in on it so that I can make it much easier for you? Having a baby as a Dhampir is much more painful than having one as a human."

"I promise I will. Oh Mom isn't he just amazing? He has my dark hair and Jordan's eyes."

"He is wonderful Leeha congratulations!"

"Oh, that makes you a Grandma now doesn't it?" Leeha and everyone else laugh so hard I think they might break all the windows.

"Ok, stop it, yes I guess that does make me a Grandma. Keep in mind all of you, of how fast our babies grow. You could be a Grandma next year as well Leeha dear." Everyone stops laughing now and they all realize that what I have said is way to true.

"Wow, I really hadn't thought about it like that. I am guessing that we should maybe slow down having too many babies too close together then. Otherwise, we will have a lot of mouths to feed and not enough food." Carrie chimes in. I read her mind about her thoughts of having children with Anthony.

"Well if we get our vamp victims, and take them back to the lab, I do believe I have figured out how to make us our own food." Jacob says calmly but is about to burst inside with enthusiasm.

"Jacob that is wonderful. Jordan and the boys can find and capture, however many you need. We just need a way to get them down into the lab without drawing to much attention to ourselves." I tell Jacob this as I too try to hide my excitement.

"Oh Mom, just leave that up to us, and you just worry about taking care of our newest family members." Grady sounds so much like a man in charge that I can't argue with him.

"Ok son, I will let you take care of it. But please be careful? I couldn't bare to lose anyone else." Grady is starting to show that he is quite the leader. I know that if anything ever happened to me that he would take very good care of this family. It just goes to show that the apple truly doesn't fall far from the tree!

Chapter Eighteen
Making Our Own Way

I agree that we should all go to the lab. That way we are all still together, and I can be there if I am needed. The trip to Justin and Nathan's house is a little longer this time. We have brought a lot of things with us and the babies slow us down a bit. I worry that if we are caught like this, we could be killed. On the other hand, they could capture us and take us to the Originals, and then we would be in an even worse state. Thankfully, we make it to the house without any trouble. The guys take everything that they need down to the lab, as the girls and I set up house. The babies are hungry so Leeha, and I feed them. The more they feed from us, the more we need to feed.

"Dan, I think Leeha and I are going to need to go on a food run. The babies are just so hungry we can't keep up if we don't eat ourselves." I don't want to leave the babies but Leeha, and I have to eat.

"I know the boys have already gone to get some food for you girls. Daddy Jordan wants to be a good husband and take care of his wife." Dan laughs remembering when I first had Anthony. "I tried to tell him that you girls would want to go get your own food, but he took Andrew, Grady and Leham, and off they went to bring the two of you something to eat. Plus, it is good practice run on getting them here to the lab. You should know better by now my love that Dhampir men have to earn our keep around here somehow."

"Why didn't you tell me so that I could have stopped them?" I am very upset with my husband for letting them go without telling me.

"Hold on love, you know that it would have just been a fight between you and Grady about him being able to do this without you. And you are the one who said that it would have to be Grady, who takes out Persia. You can't tell him that he is the strongest, and then treat him like a little baby. So I did what any Dad would do and let him be the man we all know he is! Mikatta, I love you and I would never do anything to upset you. You can't keep treating him like he is twelve." I know what my Husband says is true. I can't keep treating him like he is a child, when I know that he is quit a wonderful, and strong young man.

"You're right I am sorry for getting upset. I am his Mom, and I will always worry about him. Even though he is the strongest Dhampir that is out there. How long ago did they leave?" I am worried that it might have been a while ago, and something might be wrong. I know I can link up with them, but I don't want to be a distraction if nothing is wrong.

"They left about thirty minutes ago. It takes at least that much time for Jordan to find the vamps dear. Don't worry Crysta is keeping an eye on them so to speak. She has been looking into their futures from the second they left. But don't tell Grady that, he would be really pissed if he knew we were tracking them." Dan tells me this because he knows that I might say something when they get back. And Grady needs to know that we trust and have faith in him.

"Don't worry honey! I will not say a word. I understand the male ego dear." I wink at him and turn to go tell Leeha what is going on. Before I can get two feet from Dan, Grady and the boys come through the door, each one with two vamps in hand.

"We are taking them to the lab first. Mom, get Leeha you each get two vamps to eat now. I can't have my sister and nephew going hungry." They waste no time and he and the boys race to the lab with the vamps. I go get Leeha and the babies, and we head to the lab as well. We enter the lab to find that Jacob has made a lot of changes. He has fashioned cages that are too strong for the vamps to get out of. He has all these tubes that he is going to hook up to the vamps that Leeha and I don't eat, so he can drain them of some of their blood. Inside the cages the vamps have been chained very tightly with their arms and legs apart so they can't fight when the tubes are in.

"Mikatta, Leeha, these four are for you. We have left, them unchained so you can have a little fun with them." Jacob finds humor in the fact that we will have no problem taking out these lesser vamps. And that we will have a little fun doing so. I give Kelana to Dan, and Leeha gives Kyle to Jordan. We smile at each other and pick a cage. I step in first and the vamp thinks that he can take me, so he jumps at me. I am all to ready for him and toss him to the side with one hand. He hits the side of the cage and is dazed. I stand there waiting for him to get back up and give it another try. Leeha's vamp isn't as confident about being able to take her after seeing what I did to his friend. So he tries to keep away from her, but she is a new mother and very hungry. She catches the vamp and sinks in her teeth and starts to drain the vamp of its life. Mine had gotten back to his feet and thinks that maybe talking would be a way out. Before he can even try to speak, I am at his throat. I too am a new Mother, and I am also very hungry, I don't want to hear him beg for his life either. We step out of the cages and laugh it seems we have gotten a little messy with our meals. Still hungry, we both step into our second vamps cages. Mine knows her fate and kneels in front of me.

"If I am to die this day I am glad that it is by you Mikatta."

"How do you know my name? Did you hear my family talking about me?"

"No you are the one who killed Hanzi. And if you can kill him then I am honored that you are the one to take my life as well. I never wanted to be a vampyer. I am glad you can end this nightmare for me." She tilts her head to the side and places her hands behind her back. I did not think for one minute that she was just going to let me kill her but, I let her think that I did. As soon as I was close enough for her to strike, she jumps at me with her hands heading for my throat. I reach out my hand and catch her throat instead.

"Sorry dear but tonight you really are going to die at my hands." I sink my teeth in, as she still tries to fight me off. She scratches me more than once on my arms, and I am done with this one. I drain her quickly. Leeha doesn't give her vamp any chance to speak. She is on top of her and drinking. We both come out feeling very full and strong. I feel a little bit guilty because none of the others are eating tonight.

"What about the rest of you? I am sure that you are all very hungry as well?" I know that they are hungry because I can read it in their minds.

"Mikatta, don't worry this process shouldn't take but about a day or two. I know that this lab is stocked with those packets. For now the rest of us will use those. You and Leeha need the real thing for the babies. At their rate of growth, I am sure that they will be eating nonstop." Jacob shows so much concern for our wellbeing, which I can't help but start to feel that he is finding, is place in this family. I feel as if he is like a brother to me.

"Thank you Jacob. I know that you are going as fast as you can to get us what we need. I just don't like the fact that everyone else has to drink the packets, while Leeha and I got the real thing tonight. We all need to be at full strength, not only Leeha and me."

"Speaking as a Dad here I am glad that you and Leeha got to feed. Kyle is going to need that from her. Anthony drank both your milk and your blood. You feed a lot more during this time, so that they can get what they need. We all want these babies to be healthy so stop worrying about the rest of us and come feed these two." Jordan has found a voice that I never knew that he had, now that he is a Dad.

"Ok, ok, but I am the Mom for all of you, and I can't help it. I think "Worry" should be my new middle name." We all laugh as Leeha and I take Kelana and Kyle and let them feed now.

"Not to be rude but I could work faster if there were less of us in the lab." Jacob uses that soft suggestion that maybe those of us who are not really helping should leave. We laugh and take our leave of the lab.

Back at the house the family all sit in the living room while the babies eat. Everyone is talking about how great it would be if Jacob can really make us blood that will keep us strong and keep us alive. I too hope that he can do it. I hate putting any of our family at risk. I finish feeding Kelana and lay her in her crib next to Kyle. I sensed them before they were even four miles from the house and link to everyone so that they can feel them as well. Crysta, Dawn, Jordan, and Dan stand in front of Leeha and the babies. I stand at the front almost next to Dawn.

"Now will be a great time to show the rest of the family your gifts Dawn." I have seen her control, and I know that she could send them down the tunnel and Grady, and Andrew can take it from there.

"How many are there Mom?" I hear Leham call from the tunnel.

"At least eight that I can sense right now I am trying to read their minds. I want to know what they want from us. I want to know if they are coming here under Bell's orders, or if they are just coming here because they were passing by and smelled us."

"If we can capture them Mikatta it would be that much better. But if anyone needs to eat then by all means chow down." Jacob is always trying to be the funny guy.

"Leeha be a dear and get the door for me. I would really hate for them to break it down." Everyone laughs, the thought that I was thinking of them breaking the door just made them all relax a little.

"No problem Mom." Leeha opens the door from behind all of us. She stays really close to the babies.

The vamps come walking in as if the live here, and then they just stop dead in their tracks when they see me and Dawn standing there in front of all the rest of our family.

"You don't belong here! This is not your home, where are Nathan and Justin? They would never just leave this house. And who are you?" The oldest male vamp is the one with all the questions, so I answer them for him. It seems that they were coming here to see Nathan and Justin. Good to know that news doesn't travel to fast in the vampyer world.

"Yes we do belong here now. This is no longer Nathan and Justin's house. Two of my children and I killed them. So they had no choice but to leave you see? Now I have allowed you in because some of my children haven't eaten in a few days and well, you are what they are craving." No one moves a muscle, not us, not the vamps. Everything seems to stop just for a second. I know that we need to be the ones to strike first, so through our link, I tell Dawn to bring the wind to the vamps and to help them off of their feet. And with easy Dawn does as I ask Leeha knows where I want these vamps to go, and she sends them with the Dawn's help down to the tunnel. We all follow keeping control of the vamps. I build up a little energy just in case one gets free. I stop and turn and run back to the babies, Jordan and Dan are at my heels. There standing next to my grandson and daughter are three lesser vamps.

"IF YOU TOUCH THEM, I WILL KILL YOU!" I cannot hold back the anger and the rage that seeing them near the babies has brought to me.

"Why do you keep these things alive and not eat them?"

"Because they are our children. And if you don't move away from them, you will not live another second!" The energy I have built up is so large I am afraid that I might hurt the babies with it when I let it go. Leeha is behind me all of a sudden.

"Don't worry Mom I got the babies. Show these pisses of dust what you can do." Leeha has the crib in her mind, and will move it as soon as I need her to.

"Last chance to leave! No? Well then say goodbye." With that I let all the energy out. All three lessers vamps vanish into nothing as the energy hits them. Leeha and I have our babies in our arms before the dust clears. We check every hair and finger and toes. Kelana tells me in our special way . . .

"Momma, I am fine. So is Kyle, I was going to give them a bolt of electricity right before you came in. Momma, you are fast. How did you know they were here?"

"I could sense you and what you were seeing. You showed me that you needed me. So I came as fast as I could. I will never let anything hurt you my sweet child, or your cousin or anyone else in our family."

"Ok that is enough of the vamps. I am setting up another security system, so we can stop them before they get that close again. We need this house safe and secure." Dan seems just a little frazzled at the whole night. But we did manage to get the other eight vamps down into their cages. And Jacob says that those who haven't eaten should get at least half of one the vamps to keep our strength up. Even he has a little dinner.

It has only been a week and Jacob is already starting to make the blood that he believes that we will be able to live off of. He wants to be the one to try the blood, but I won't let him.

"Mikatta I made it I should test it!" He is almost yelling at me at this point.

"Jacob, if something goes wrong, who here knows how to help you? None of us and you know how much we need you to keep working on this, so I will try the blood."

"NO!" It comes from all of my family.

"Are you crazy Mom?" Grady asks.

"No way are we risking you." Jordan adds.

"Look, I am the one who should try it. I can link to all of you to draw energy if I need to keep myself alive. I can give you the time you would need to get me one of the real vamps for me to drink from. Besides you are all insane if you think that I would let anyone of you take such a risk. I have more power inside me than any of you, and I am going to be the one drinking it. End of discussion! Jacob give me the blood!"

Dan takes the glass from Jacob and walks over to me and hands me the glass.

"Don't you dare die on me." He says holding me in his arms.

"I have no intentions of going anywhere. Jacob is a very good doctor, and I know that he has made us our new drink of choice." I take the glass and drink the entire thing. Everyone waits and watches me very closely. The blood has a very real vamp blood taste to it. And I do not feel anything wrong. In fact, I feel energized. I have the same feeling that I get when I drink from a real vamp. "Jacob, my dear brother, this is even better than drinking the vamps. You did it!" I run and hug him as tight as I can. Finally, we have found something that will keep as alive and keep us full.

Chapter Nineteen
Another Meeting

Now that we have our new food supply, and we don't have to go out of our way as much to find food, we are back at the Ranch trying to get a game plan. We don't have to go far to find food, so we know we are going to have to build up our strength, for when Persia decided to come for me. Grady and Andrew were working on there fighting skills, as everyone else was also practicing on their own gifts and making sure that we all had complete control of them. Kyle and Kelana are four weeks old now and look as if they are four. They seem to be growing much faster than Anthony did. I think it might have to do with the new food that we are eating. Jacob thinks that the additives that he has to use might be like an accelerant for the kids. Kyle has found his gift finally. Kyle the little boy can start fires. This comes in handy for Dawn. He starts the fire for her, and she can make it do whatever she wants it to.

So far, no new Dhampirs have shown up, and not that I don't think we would have a better chance with more of us, but I don't think I can take any more Dhampirs right now. We have been running through different scenarios of how it might go down with Persia. Jordan and Leham have been going out during the day and looking for where Persia has gotten off to. So far, they haven't been able to find any trace of him.

Anthony and Carrie have fallen in love and it scares me so much. Even Leham and Crysta still have not talked about marriage and kids and what their lives will be like. Anthony and Carrie talk about it a lot. I don't think that I am ready for him to get married. He truly is only eight months old, even in my heart that is how I feel about him. Carrie sees the man that he is right now, not the child that he is. I want to say something to them about waiting, but I know it wouldn't really do any good. I know the love they feel for each other is just as deep as the love I have for Dan or the love Jordan and Leeha have. That doesn't change the fact that he hasn't really lived life like Carrie has. All he has known so far is death and fighting. Yes, he has seen life be born, and he has even had the chance for new family members to come into his life. I just am not ready for him to be a man just yet.

I decided that I need a nice hot bath, and hand Kelana to Dan. I close the door and try to disconnect from the family. I just need to only be in my own thoughts right now. I sit down and close my eyes as I let the hot water, and bubbles relax me.

"Mikatta, you need to speak with Belle again!" There is that figure again and that voice, this time I talk back.

"Why? Because you want me to? I don't even know if I should be listening to you. Having the babies is not safe for us. I would have never aloud it, yet you said that we were going to have them. Why would you give us more to deal with?"

"Mikatta I know that you don't doubt me. And your questions are all valid. The children are needed for what you are going to have to come up against very soon. And you have handled everything that you have had to come up against. I have not brought all of this pain and death to you only your gifts and bringing you all together. I knew that the Vampyers were getting to strong for the world. Justin was my only way to bring you to life my dear. Justin was turned against his will, and he had a good heart. So I used him to make you."

"So you are the one that really made us? That is why Crysta and Grady didn't get a lot of bad things from Justin when they killed him. Why did you let us kill him if he was good?"

"Justin was still a vampyer, and he wanted to kill humans. He knew he needed to die. And who else would he want to do that but you Mikatta?"

"Why do you want me to talk to Belle? What good would that do? She wants to breed us so that she can have her own child, like I have."

"Mikatta, you know you are stronger than them. And you can still block your thoughts from her. Dan and Leeha can help. Belle must believe that you are alone. She will be alone soon so you should get ready. You will know when the time is right."

"I have done everything that you have asked of me. So I will do this for you. So I have to ask one thing from you. Please keep my family safe. Losing Kara has really hurt are family."

"I have protected your family Mikatta. Kara made her own choose and her own sacrifice for the family."

I opened my eyes, and the figure is gone. I really wish I felt like I was this strong person the figure keeps saying that I am. I know when the time comes I will become this wicked powerful Dhampir. I am not sure I can take out another Original. I get out of the tub and get dressed. I go out to tell Dan and Leeha what has happened to me.

"So we are supposed to help keep her from seeing into your mind, is that right?" Leeha asks me with true concern.

"That is what he said, or at least, it sounds like a he. Any ways, he says I will know when the time was right. And I am getting that feeling that now is the time to do this. I think I should go to the woods to do as well."

"Ok we will stay inside the house, and we will keep the shield up around your mind." Dan says this like he isn't sure about doing this whole thing.

"I need to get into hers, just keep her out of mine ok?"

"You got it Mom. Don't worry we got your back."

I go out to the back of the Ranch. I know that I can connect to her because she has been trying to get inside my head all this time. I get far enough away from the ranch so when I connect with Belle, I am the only one that she will be able to reach with her mind reading. I sit down and close my eyes. I think only of Belle.

"Well, well Mikatta, I never thought that you would get into my mind. Funny, I am having a little trouble getting into yours? Now why is that?"

"Belle you need to stop this! We are not going to let you mate with us. We are stronger then you know, and I am telling you that you should stop trying to find us."

"I will find you and we will mate with your family. And I will have a child of my own."

"Belle, please stop this. You will never be able to get to us. I will never let you hurt my family! Stay away from us.

I will kill you if you try to get too even one of my family members."

"No, Mikatta I will not give up. You have your family. I was created, and I am not ever going to be able to have children. My mate made us and even he can't have children of his own. I do not know how you can be like us, yet you can have a family." I understand now what it is that Belle is after. I will never let her anywhere near any of my family just so that she can have an evil child.

"Belle, I am only going to say this one last time. You will never get anywhere near my family. I have already stopped two of you from doing so."

"Not true Mikatta, Persia did kill one of you." Belle sounds very smug about the fact that Persia killed Kara. I remember what the Figure said to me.

"Kara made a sacrifice for our family. Persia was knocked on his ass! And if I hadn't stopped my son, Persia would be dead right now. So if you think for even one minute that what happened to Kara had anything to do with Persia, think again. She made a sacrifice, for her family. Can you say that any of your originals would do that for you?" I know that this has hurt Belle. They are not a family, and they are only out for self-perseveration. This truly angers Belle that I know so much about them.

"I know longer want to speak with you Mikatta . . ." And just like that I could no longer read Belle.

"You ok Mom?" Leeha comes off the porch to make sure that I am unharmed.

"I am fine dear. At least now we know what Belle is after. I think that she is going to send Persia after us again. I have made her very mad. After that conversation, I know that she will not let my arrogance go unpunished. We need to be ready for this. I do not believe that she will only send Persia this time."

We tell the rest of the family what has happened, and we start to prepare for our upcoming battle. With Kelana and Kyle still so young we know that we are going to have to keep them somewhere safe. I know that Jacob is very important to us, and that we can't let anything happen to him. So Jacob and the children will go to the lab when all this goes down. Grady wants a second chance at killing Persia. He wants to drain him of all his life's blood. Part of it is because of what he did to Kara. The other part is because he knows that Persia is after me. I am really worried about what other Original's that will be coming with him. We have been practicing all different types of battles, but when you don't know what to expect, well you just have to go with whatever comes at you.

The blood that Jacob has made for us has done perfectly for keeping us feed and safe at home. We only have to find one or two vamps every now and then to make more of our food. This new food has made Kelana and Kyle grow much faster than Anthony did. Anthony has stopped aging, and if I had to say what age he was I would say around twenty five. Carrie and Anthony do not spend any time away from each other. Yet they have kept themselves from taking their relationship any further at this time. I know that they are only waiting until all of this Persia business is over with. Then I will have to deal with their feelings for each other. Dan has been at my side from the minute that all this started, and I know he will never leave me. Every chance that he gets, he takes me in his arms and holds on tight to me and kisses me. He tells me not to forget how much I mean to him, and that he could never love anyone the way that he loves me. I feel as if he thinks that something might happen to him or me during all this. I remind him that we have a much greater power than the Originals. We have family! And as if he didn't know this already our family bond is so strong that we won't allow anything to happen to each other. Our love for each other is what keeps our strength up. There is no other power as strong as love. We will use that strength to defeat them. I told Belle that I will not let her near my family, and I mean to hold to that.

Weeks have gone by and still no attacks from Persia. I can feel the tension building in my family. They are worried that he will attack, and we won't be ready for him.

"Everyone listen to me please. I know that we are all on edge here. The waiting is always the hardest part in something like this. But, as I have told Dan, our love for each other as a family is what makes us so strong. I don't believe that he is going to attack us here. We are way to guarded, and we have the advantage. We are going to have to go out on a hunt for Persia to come to us. I know where he is waiting for us. Crysta has seen how many of them, there are, and this time I am going to take care of all the lesser vamps before they have a chance to try and distract any of us from our main purpose. After that I want us all to remain connected, and NO ONE is to go off on their own trying to be a hero! Our power is in our connection. This is going to be a battle of strengths. Grady and Andrew, Persia is your main target, you two stay together, and we will keep everything else out of your way. I know that we will be able to kill Persia. My concern is that Belle isn't going to only send Persia at us this time. She will be sending another one of the Originals with him. I can't see who she is sending, so that means I don't what gift that this one will have. So, everyone must stay focused. I know that all of us can do this, and everyone will be coming home together." I know I have said a lot, but I think they all need to hear what I believe.

"Your right Mom, if we stay connected and work together we can do this." Jordan stands up and walks up to me and hugs me.

"Yea Mom, we got this shit!" Grady runs and tries to tackle me with his hug. I am not going down that easy.

"It is in the bag Mom." Anthony hugs me as well.

"Ok then, we are going to have to leave the Ranch for this battle to happen. I want us all to stay close together. And no one disconnects form the link. I want to be able to know what is happening to everyone." With this I send Jacob and the kids to the lab, with a prayer that God will keep them safe. We start out on our search for Persia and his little band of vamps. We are about half a day away from the Ranch when I sense him, and if I can sense him, I know he can sense us as well. I bring everyone to a stop, and we form a circle. I have begun to build all the energy that I can inside of me, and I seek out all the lesser vamps. Anthony knows what I need to do with all my energy, and waits until I am ready for him. Suddenly, all the lesser vamps come at us from all around. I let out my energy, and Anthony projects it to all of the lesser vamps. They all disappear into nothing. Persia comes out into the open so that we can see him. At the moment, he is alone, but I can sense another close by. I still can't tell which one of them it is.

"Well, Mikatta I see you are ready for me this time. No bother, I will still take your life from you. And I believe that I would love to take your son's life as well!"

"Persia there is something I believe that my son would like to show you!"

Grady breaks from the circle, but at the same time without Persia knowing it Andrew breaks from behind us. Anthony and I take all the power that I can from everyone of our family members, except Dawn. She is going to be a wonderful distraction for the second Original, who seems to think that we do not know that they are here. Grady comes faces to face with Persia, and I am ready with all the energy, and Anthony is ready to help me send it out. We stay in our circle without Andrew and Grady.

Persia smiles and then takes a swing at my son, which Grady has no problem ducking from, while at the same time he hits Persia right in the stomach and sends him flying about twenty feet, where he sees for the first time my other son Andrew. Andrew draws back his leg and sends a kick that is so hard to Persia's head it spins him around on his back four times. By this time Grady is next to Andrew.

"I am sorry. I should have introduced you to my brother here. Persia, meet my brother Andrew." With that both Andrew and Grady begin to beat on Persia without any mercy. Back and forth, they work on him. Blood is pouring out of Persia, and Grady can't wait any longer, and he bites down on Persia's neck. Andrew holds Persia, as he tries to fight off Grady. I can feel the power that my son is gaining from the blood of this Original. As soon as Grady has drained Persia of his last drop of blood, and he turns to dust, Samuel Pope steps out of the shadows. Before I can do anything to stop him, he sends a gust of wind so strong, it knocks Andrew and Grady at least fifty feet away from us. I try to build up my energy to send at Samuel but Anthony sends it to Dawn instead. Dawn calls the earth from underneath Samuel's feet, and the ground opens up and Samuel falls in. Dawn quickly closes the hole.

"I don't think we are ready to fight this one lets go while we can." Dawn tells all of us. I call everyone to me, and we start our return to home.

Chapter Twenty
New Knowledge

Back at the lab, we fill Jacob in on all that we have just gone through. I am glad that he and the kids were not there with us during this battle. I don't think I would have been able to focus with them there.

"Awwww, you guys had all the fun!" Jacob sounds like he truly wishes that he could have been there.

"You know that you are the only one of us that can make our food. If anything was to happen to you, we would be right back where we were. You are not someone that we can risk Jacob." I hope that he understands how important that he is to our family. "We need you brother."

"I know. I just wish that I could have at least seen it."

"Well now that is something I can help you with Uncle." Crysta takes Jacobs hands and closes her eyes. Jacob feels a shock, and his eyes close. Crysta shows her new Uncle everything that happened to us, not leaving anything out.

"Wow, Grady and Andrew are you two ok? That looked like it really hurt." He says with a little sarcasm.

"We are golden man. I am so proud of our family. Taking out Persia was the best thing we could have done. They no longer have that power boost." Grady is still glowing from drinking Persia's blood.

Grady now has the knowledge that Persia had in him. Samuel Pope can control all the elements, just like Dawn. Now we have to figure out how to kill him. I know that he didn't stay inside the ground, seeing he too can control it. I know that we will not have to worry about being attack by any of the vamps anytime soon. Killing Persia has set them back just a bit. I can now focus on raising Kelana, and teaching her how to use her gift. My other problem is that Anthony has proposed to Carrie, and of course, she has said yes. So now we are planning a wedding as well.

I remember both of my wedding days. I couldn't have been happier than I was at those moments. Why was I not feeling those same feelings right now with Carrie marrying my son? I walk into the room where Carrie is getting ready and have to stop. Carrie looks so beautiful. I can't even move. Carrie turns around, and she sees me staring at her.

"Do I look ok?"

"Oh Carrie, dear you look amazing. I don't think I have seen anyone so beautiful on their wedding day. Well, other than Leeha and myself." I smile and walk up to her and hug her. "You know that I have not really been happy about you and Anthony making this decision. Even though it isn't a legal marriage, is God's eyes it will be. I have to tell you something, Anthony in still just a baby to me. You have lived a full life. He has only been alive for nine months. You have experienced so much more than he has. I wanted so much for him before he fell in love. I never thought that he would marry the very first woman he fell in love with. And I know that we are different now, but it doesn't change the fact that I am worried his heart will get broken." I say all this with tears in my eyes.

"I promise you that I will never break Anthony's heart. I have lived a longer life than he has, but he grows and learns in a much different way than we did. He knows what he is feeling, and he knows what it is that he wants. We will have the same troubles as any other couple, but we will have all of you to help us through them. I love Anthony like I have never loved any man ever before. I give him my heart, my soul, and all of me." Now I have Carrie crying.

"I know dear. I can read you very well. But I will always worry about him. You will just have to understand that about me. I am going to go see my son. Oh and by the way, Dan was wondering if he could walk you down the aisle?"

"I . . . . I . . . don't know what to say, I mean YES! I would love it if he would walk me down the aisle." This has made Carrie very happy and there are no more tears. I walk into Anthony's room, and I see my baby, dressed in a tux, looking so very grown up. I hold back all the tears so that I can try and talk to my son.

"You look wonderful Anthony. I wanted to talk to you a little bit if I could?"

"Of course Mom, you know that you can say anything to me. I think that you and I both know that the bound that we have is something most mother and sons don't have."

"Thank you son, and you're right, we do have a special bond. And it is that bond I have to speak about. You are still a baby to me, and I am having a very hard time with you getting married already. Carrie is the first woman that you have loved. I know that feeling is very strong, and that it is hard not to take things slow. But you are different than most young men, and you have learned things, and know things that well, you just shouldn't yet. I just need to hear it from you, without me reading your mind that this is truly what you really want."

"Mom, I love you so much, I love the way you worry about all of us all the time. Most of all I love that I was giving to you as your son. I couldn't have been given to two better parents. I love Carrie in a way I can't explain to anyone. I know you understand what I mean. Your marriage to your first husband Kevin, and now to my wonderful dad Dan, tells me you know love. So yes Mom, this is what I want. I want to marry Carrie and start our lives together so that someday we too can have our own family." Anthony stands tall, walks over to me, and picks me up in a gentle hug. I hug him right back, still trying not to show all those tears that I have inside just bursting to be let out. It is time for us to go. We walk out to the barn, which has been transformed into the most beautiful wedding scene. Jordan is acting as our Pastor, and he so looks the part. He has been researching how this is supposed to go and has gotten very good at reciting the ceremony. Everyone is ready, Carrie walks in on Dan's arm and everything feels right all of a sudden in my heart.

We hold a little wedding reception with cake, gifts and dancing. This is the first time that I believe we as a family have been able to completely relax and not worry about anyone attacking us.

Grady and I sit down together and go over what it is that he has learned from Persia. The remaining ten are very worried that we can and will kill them all. They also are not all wanting the same thing that Belle wants. They don't all want to mate with us and have children. That information could really help us when and if any of us get captured, and Belle tries to mate with any of us. They may not want to have kids with us, but all the rest still want us dead. This Samuel Pope is going to be really tricky to kill. Like Dawn, he can control the elements. And from what we have seen with Dawn that is not something that we really know how to fight. Having Dawn with us will be helpful. We will need to get close to him to kill him, and that will be hard with him being able to control the wind and the earth. His power for fire is the same as Dawn's, if there is no fire, he can't just create it out of nowhere. Grady and I agree that we need to start training Dawn on how to fight Samuel. But even we aren't sure how to train her, how do you train someone if you don't have the gifts needed to do so. We will sit down and talk to Dawn about what we know and maybe her understanding Samuel will be enough to help her prepare.

I haven't been for a night walk in a very long time. I tell the family that I am going to go for a walk. Of course, they all want to know if they can come with me, but I simple tell them I need to clear my head. Dan takes my hand, kisses me and tells me . . .

"Please my love be safe out there. Don't go far from us, just because we have killed Persia, doesn't mean that they won't still send the lessers after us."

"I am always alert my love, you know that. I won't go far I just need some time to myself in the night air. After everything that we have been through in the last month, I really need to be alone. I have my link if I need any of you. I love you for worrying about me so much it shows your soft side." I tickle him a little and laugh. Then I give him a kiss, and I walk out the door.

The night air always seems to have a way of wrapping me in comfort. The smell that it brings and the sounds that you can hear are very relaxing to me. I walk for about an hour, just in a circle around the Ranch, so that I can keep to my word about not going far. Suddenly, the smell in the air changes, I smell a human very close by. I stop and duck down in the grass. I look with my Dhampir eyes to see where this human is. Just about eighty feet from the left of me, I see him. His is a short man, looks like he shaves his head. This human has many tattoos on his body. In his hand is a wooden stake! I realize that he must be a vampyer hunter. Then the panic hits. He thinks that we are vampyers. I read his mind . . . he has come here with three other hunters, they have tracked us. They believe that maybe we are a new breed of vampyer, and that we should be stop while there are still few of us. It only takes me a split second to move myself right in front of him and remove the stake from his hand.

"Please, I am not a vampyer, and I do not wish to kill you, or for you to kill me or any of my family! My name is Mikatta Hope. I am a Dhampir. We were created from good not evil. We have been killing the vampyers, and we have also managed to kill two of the Original twelve."

"What do you mean you are a Dhampir? And no hunter or even a lesser vamp can kill one of the Originals."

"If you and your friends promise not to try and hurt us, I promise none of my family will harm any of you as well." Just as I say these words all of my family are right at my back. The Hunter's eyes are about the size of golf balls at this moment.

"Everyone come out, and give your weapons to Mikatta. We promise not to try and hurt any of you. But you will have to tell us everything about you. And I do mean everything!" We take the vamp hunters back to the Ranch. It takes us about an hour to get there. Only because they are human and cannot run as fast as us. I tell them I will not speak about us until we are back at our home, and everyone can feel safer.

"Ok, before I tell you any more about us you are going to have to tell me your names." I hate not knowing someone's name that I am talking to.

"Oh, of course I am so sorry. My name is Jason and this is Rick. The fat one there is Jake, and our youngest hunter is Matt. We have been hunting the lesser vamps, since we were children, just like our fathers and their fathers and so on and so on. It is passed down to each generation. We have no problem killing the lesser vamps, but we have no way of being able to kill the Originals. Their powers are too great. We stay as far away from them as we can. We think of ourselves as the border patrol. We try to keep their lesser vamp's numbers down. So now that you know about us, please tell us about you and how you killed two of the Originals?"

I begin our tale from the very beginning. Making sure that I don't leave anything out. They listen with such passion

I can read in their minds that they believe everything that I am telling them.

"So you have a heart beat? You can walk in the day? And you have gifts just like the Originals? I don't know what to say, it would be an honor if you would allow us to fight alongside you?" Jason seems to be the leader, and I find his eagerness a refreshing trait.

"I think that you fighting alongside us might be a little difficult. See we can move very, very fast. It only took us an hour to walk to the Ranch because we were walking at your pace. My family was at the Ranch when I called them to help me with all of you. It only took them a minute to get to us. We have watched one of our own die. I don't think I could stand to see any human be killed by any of those vamps, just because we were unable to protect you."

"Ok, but can we at least try and work together somehow? I know with the knowledge we have and the knowledge you have gained. We could take out these vampyers." Jason's heart is a good one, and I do think there could be a way for us to work together.

"You know the lab I was telling you about?"

"Yea the one that was used by the two vamps that helped make you all."

"Yes, well it is hard for us to be there and here. I would like it if you went with Jacob and Jordan to the lab. I believe that you would be great protection for them. I also believe that Rick, there could learn how to make our blood."

"How did you know that Rick has medical knowledge?" Jason still doesn't understand the gifts we have.

"I know that and he has had a really hard time finding the right girl. He just can't seem to find one that can handle his child-like ways." I laugh as Rick's face turns bright red.

"Right you can read minds. And I think if it means that we can help you in this fight then we will be happy to help you in any way possible."

"Thank you. You are all welcome to stay the night here and rest. You have been tracking us for days. I have another question, are there more of you out there?"

"Oh yea, the vamps are not just here they are all over the world. This is only a fraction of our team. We only brought four because we were not really sure that you were vampyers. We thought you might just be a new breed and that there wouldn't be very many of you. We figured that we could easily kill you. I see now that we were very mistaken!" He and his entire group laugh.

It has been a long time since we have been around humans. I am glad that we can still behave normally enough not to scare them. Meeting Jason and his crew has been very refreshing. Jason is about five-foot and five-inches tall, with no hair only because he shaves it, has brown-eyes and is tatted up really good. He seems the type that likes really loud music and loves a good fight. But he has this sense of honor about him, like if I were to ask him to stay with us and fight with us, I know that he feels that it is his duty to do so and he would stay. He also has the sickest sense of humor, but he makes me laugh, and that is something that we don't really get to do around here a lot. Rick is taller I am thinking maybe five-feet and nine-inches, dark-brown hair and brown-eyes. He seems the real quiet type, until he really feels comfortable, and then he is not so quiet. He is very strange, and I am not so sure that he thinks on the same wave length as the rest of us. Then we have Jake, as Jason called him the fat one. He is a bit on the chunky side, but he is also about six-feet tall with dirty blonde hair. He seems to be the strong silent type. The whole time we were talking he just sits and listens. But I read right into him. He is very smart and knows a lot more than what his fellow vampyer hunters know. I won't tell his secret to them, but I am going to talk to him myself about it. Last but not least, we have Matt. Matt likes to talk, about anything but himself. He stays in the conversation just fine as long as you don't ask him any questions about him. I have to say I think Matt might be a little bit on the oriental side. Not too tall, around five-feet and five-inches, black-hair and average for his weight size. I don't like to look into people's minds that I respect. I have learned not to read any of my families minds, unless we are linked. I don't always like what I see. But I want to know everything that these four know about the vampyers.

Their families have been fighting them for decades. They have to know something about where the Originals would be living. I know that they move from place to place, but they must have some sort of a pattern that the hunters must know, if they always try to stay clear of them. It is getting late, and I can sense that the four of them need rest. We have almost forgotten that they are still humans. I show Jason and Rick to a room with a bathroom, so they can clean up and even give them some of the boys' clothes to wear. Then I do the same for Jake and Matt. We all tell them goodnight, and we go back to the family room where we always sit and talk before we spend our own alone time.

"I think that is really wicked that we have met these vampyer hunters. I know that there is a lot that we can learn from them, and a lot that they can learn from us as well. Imagine, their families have been fighting the vampyers for decades. They have to know some things that we haven't gotten the time or chance to learn about them just yet." I am over excited and just ramble.

"Yea, I really like Jason. Do you think that we can get tattoos?" Leham seems very intrigued by all the tattoos that Jason has, and I think he might just want to be a little bit more like him personality wise as well.

"I have no idea and I don't really think that you should go running off and getting something like that on a whim dear son." Dan looks at Leham with that very stern father face.

"Ok, ok I know, but you have to admit that he is really cool."

"Yes he is a pretty interesting person. I do want to get to know them all better." Dan has his concerns about how we will be able to work together with the vampyer hunters, with them being human and all.

"I know that we all have the same concerns about them being human, and if we can protect them and still fight the same way we have. But if you think about it, this is what they do. They fight the vampyers all the time without being anything but human."

"Mom is right this is a good thing that we have met with them. I did try to look into their pasts, but I didn't feel right about doing it without asking permission." Crysta has the same feelings as I do about intruding on someone that we like and respect with asking if we can.

"Ok everyone, I think we all need to rest up a bit, and take some time to ourselves." We have had such a full day I want to be alone with my husband and kids. It is the only time that I ever feel just a little normal.

Chapter Twenty One
Someone from the Past

We have spent the past week with the four vampyer hunters, talking and learning. It is time for them to get back to their families for a little while to let them know what they are going to be up to. We have decided that they should come stay with us for at least a few months. We really need for Jacob to spend some real time at the lab, and he needs to show Rick how to make our blood. I don't want to see them leave, but they don't believe that it would be the right thing to takes us back to where they live just yet. They think that their families would be worried that we might still want to drink their blood. Them going back alone and being able to tell them about us would be easier. So we agree to let them go without any of us following.

I haven't feed from a real vampyer in almost three weeks. And with nursing Kelana, I really need to feed. Leeha is feeling the same as I am, so we agree that at least she and I need to feed from some real vamps. We will take only half of the family with us. Grady will stay with the kids and the rest of the family while Dawn, Andrew, Dan and Anthony come with Leeha and me. I know now that we should have brought Jordan with us, but Leeha wanted him to stay with Kyle. It would have taken a lot less time to find the vamps. We must have searched for hours. I finally had to link to Crysta and ask her to look into the future and see if we might ever find something to eat.

"Mom you know I can't tell that. I only see the things that are to help us." She tells me in a motherly voice.

"Well, we might be a little while then. I can't sense any vamps."

"You just need to relax Mom you are to hungry, and you are not letting it come to you. That is all Jordan really does." Crysta tries to calm me with her thoughts.

"Ok, I will relax, but this is still not my thing." I unlink from her and just stand still for a moment with everyone around me. We all close our eyes and let go of everything. Almost instantly we all open our eyes. We can smell them. They are at least five or six miles away. Leeha and I are so hungry that we just start running. It only takes us a moment to get to where the vamps are. There seems to be around seven of them. I don't want to just go rushing in without thinking about how we are going to take these vamps. I will not go home without even one of my family members.

"I think that we should come at them from all angles. That will keep them from getting away. And it will also take them by surprise." Dan is thinking like Grady and Andrew. "Andrew you go with Mom. I will go with Leeha. Anthony and Dawn you two are together."

"I am linking us all now. Stay open to my energy just in case you need it. Leeha and I need to feed as much as we can, but if you have to kill them please don't waste the food." We all laugh and split up, we circle around the vamps and begin to close in. As all of our attacks have been this goes very quickly, Andrew and I take on two of the vamps. One male and a female, I have no trouble feeding from the female, as Andrew holds the male for me. Dan and Leeha have two others in their hands and Leeha drinks from her first vamp.

She too is feeding from a female and Dan is holding a male in his hands. Dawn and Anthony have the other three down on the ground two males and another female. I finish with my first and take the vamp from Andrew and begin to feed again. You would not believe how hungry you get when you are a nursing Dhampir. Leeha has finished her second and we both move to the three that Dawn and Anthony have pinned to the ground. They are all lying on their stomachs. I turn the first one over and drain him of his blood as Leeha finishes off the female. I turn the last male over . . . Leeha and I both let out some sort of scream. Anthony understands what we are seeing in this male and he stands him up.

"NO IT ISN"T POSSIBLE! YOU'RE DEAD!" I am staring into the face of my dead husband Kevin Hope. Leeha almost passes out, but Andrew catches her. Anthony has a very tight hold on Kevin. I bring myself back to the moment and realize that Dan and the others have no idea who this vampyer is.

"I don't believe that you are standing here in front of me, Kevin, I saw you dead. We buried you in the ground!"

"You know me? And you call me Kevin?" He talks like he has no idea who I am.

"You don't know who you were before you were turned into a vampyer?" Anthony asks the question. He knows that I am having a very hard time dealing with this.

"My name is Jason that is what my maker calls me. I only know what my maker tells me."

"Who is your maker?" I have to know who turned my husband into a vampyer.

"Belle is my maker. She is also the one who I am with. She will be very unhappy with you for killing me."

"Kevin I am not going to kill you just yet. I am taking you back with us. I need to know if there is any way that we can bring back your memory." I have to know if Kevin remembers what happened to him.

I keep my mind closed to Crysta as we get closer to the Ranch with Kevin in tow. I don't want her seeing anything just yet so Dan and Leeha use the shield to block everyone else's minds as well. I can't look at him, and I am holding on very tight to Dan. I loved Kevin very much and our life together was the most wonderful time that I had while I was a human. But I am not that same woman. Dan is my soul mate, and I don't want him to think for one moment that I still have any feelings towards Kevin. I just want to know why he was chosen to be changed and why it was Belle, who did it. I remember the night that I found Kevin laying out on our sidewalk. He had gone out for a short walk. He was a computer programmer, and he spent a lot of time sitting, he did this every night. I usually would go with him, but I had been working in our garden and didn't want to stop. I hadn't realized how long that he had been gone. I was so into the garden. Then I thought I should go in and clean up so I could make us dinner. I went inside thinking that he would be sitting at his desk, but he wasn't anywhere in the house. So I called his cell phone, at first I didn't hear his phone ringing, I was at the back of our house. I got his voicemail. I knew he always took the phone with him so I called the phone again, this time I had walked out the front door. That is when I heard his phone ring, I walk to where I hear the phone, and there laid Kevin, pale white eyes wide open and laying in a lump on the sidewalk. The coroner couldn't say how long that he had been dead, something about the loss of blood made it difficult to tell. I didn't think about it then but I remember now that there was no blood anywhere around my husband. In fact, there wasn't any blood on any of his clothes. I didn't even think about it when they said that they couldn't tell the true cause of death. The police tried to find out what had happened to Kevin. They even thought that it was me that had killed him. After all their running in circles doing really nothing, they closed the case as a unknown death. We buried him the very next day after his death. Kevin had everything already planned so it went very smoothly. I spent months just crying myself to sleep over the loss of my husband. I even thought about killing myself, but Grady and Crysta knew that something was up with me and decided to move back home to take care of me. To see him now, after everything that I have been through and after everything that I have learned was a lot for me to handle. My head started to feel a little light, and everything starts to get a little hazy. Dan scoops me up in his arms and carries me the rest of the way to the Ranch.

As we get closer to the Ranch Grady and Crysta come running out to see what Crysta has seen in her vision. She screams as she sees the face of her Dad.

"YOU CAN'T BE MY DAD!" The tears are coming in streams from her face. Grady holds on to her as he looks at Kevin.

"How the hell are you alive? We buried you! You son of a bitch! The hell that you put Mom through, I should kill you for that reason alone." Grady's eyes have become a very bright purple.

"Grady he doesn't remember who he is. He thinks that his name is Jason. Belle is his maker and his lover!" I say this with the most amount of revulsion that I can. "The only reason I didn't kill him myself is because I want to know why he doesn't remember his past life. And I want to know why Belle chose him to change. Your Dad's heart was not an evil one, so why did she want him? Crysta, I know what I am about to ask you to do is going to be very difficult for you, but I really need you and I to do this. I want us to link together and try to show him his past. And if we can't do that I want to try and see into his past if it is possible."

"I don't even want to touch this disgusting piece of trash!" She looks at me and is yelling at me.

"Crysta Dawn Hope, I am not asking anymore. We will try this. It is important to all of us to know this information." I am on my feet and in my daughter's face now. She cannot challenge me. She never could.

"Put him on his knees." I tell Anthony and Andrew, they have been keeping him from running away this whole time. They force Kevin to his knees and hold him there. I take Crysta's hand even, as she tries to resist me I pull her over to him. I take my hands and hers, and we place them on his head. I have my hand on top of Crysta's so that she can't pull away from the process. I am thinking about my life with Kevin and try to start from the day we met. Letting him see what I see, but there is no reaction from him.

"Crysta you are going to have to do this because I can't."

"Fine, but this thing will never be my father ever again."

"That is not why I am asking you to do this. I want to know why Belle did this to him of all people." This time Crysta does what I could not. She shows Kevin his past life. I can tell that he can feel everything that she is giving to him, by the way, his body is shaking. I can see the things that she is showing him. I know that it is causing her so much pain to go back through our human lives.

"Ok sweetheart that is enough, you can stop now." She too is shaking and the crying hasn't stopped yet. Kevin tries to get to his feet, but my boys are too strong for him.

"Mikatta, Crysta and Grady? You were my family when I was a human?"

"Yes, we were. We are no longer your family. You need to understand that. All I want to see is what happened the night that your human life ended. Do you think that you can show me and Crysta that?"

"I don't even know what happened. I only remember what you have shown me and then there is just Belle." He seems as if he wants to remember but just can't find anything there.

"Maybe we can help you if you try. You have to want to remember it or there is nothing that Crysta, and I can do."

"I will try." Kevin closes his eyes and Crysta, and I place our hands on his head again. This time Crysta helps me to show him the last night that we shared together. I show everything that happened that night. Even I shed a few tears as we show him my memories. Kevin stands to his feet. Anthony and Andrew can't stop him. He stares at me with that look that he would when we were alone together, and he wanted me to know that he loved me.

"She changed me because she knew how much I loved you. She wanted me to love her that way. She wanted everything that you had. She wants to have your family as her own." Kevin drops to his knees and falls on his hands. "You have to kill me Mikatta. I can't go back to her. Not with these memories, she will see them and use them against you. You must kill me!" I know what he says is true, but I can't bring myself to do it. Even though I know what he is, I just can't. I link to Dan . . .

"Please, I know he must die, but I just can't be the one to do it. Help me my love!"

"You need to go to our room, and take the kids, and I mean Grady, and Crysta and Kelana. The rest of us can do this my love." I nod my head and I take the kids, and we go to my room. We can hear the rest of the family taking Kevin out to the woods. They all know how good we can hear, and Dan doesn't want us to hear them killing Kevin. I don't feel anything right now. Neither do Grady or Crysta. Kevin has not been a part of our lives for years now, and we have a new life and a wonderful new family that we love and want to be with for the rest of our lives. I can no longer hear their footsteps. I sit there and I pray that they make it quick and painless. At the same time Grady, Crysta and I all hit the floor.

"I am sorry that you had to go through that with Kevin, my dears. I wanted you to know how far back this goes." We are standing in front of the image of the man that I have been seeing in my last three visions. Only this time I am not seeing him alone. "Belle has wanted you Mikatta from the moment that she laid eyes on you. She could not get into your head. She couldn't get into Grady or Crysta's either. So she took the only thing that she could, she took Kevin and has been toying with him ever since. You are all very strong headed. You do not let anyone tell you what to do, you never have. And it is that stubbornness that has gotten you all this far. Everything about you Mikatta is what Belle has always wanted. A husband that truly loves her, children of her own, and the chance to live her own life. That is what Kevin was trying to tell you. Believe me your family killing him is the best thing that has happened to him for over two years now. I know you are confused and you all have questions. But now is not the time."

As we come to, I look to make sure that Kelana is still with us and that she is ok. But there where I left my little daughter sitting, now is a teenage beautiful girl. How long had we been out for?

"Kelana dear how long were we on the floor for?" I ask my daughter, but I don't even know if she can talk to me yet.

"Not long, maybe five minutes at the most." Her voice is sweet like honey to my ears. It soothes me in ways I do not understand.

"Do you know how it is that you have grown so fast in only those five minutes?" Again, I ask this question not knowing if I will be able to get a real answer from her.

"Yes, Mother God has been here with me and with all of you. Don't you remember him talking to you about Belle and Kevin?" All three of our mouths drop as my baby tells me about what I thought only Grady, Crysta and I had witnessed. I touch Kelanna's hand. I see what she has seen and know why she has been aged so quickly. We are going to need everyone that we have to fight the vamps that Belle is going to send after us now that Kevin is no longer hers.

"Kyle has been aged as well. And you need to get the vampyer hunters back as soon as you can. She is very pissed off that we took him back." Crysta is having a vision and has tears coming from her eyes. I believe that she has seen how Kevin, her Dad, was killed.

Dan and the others return, and I fill them in on what has happened here while they were taking care of Kevin. This has never been easy for any of us. We have all been thrown into this life, without being asked if it is what we wanted to do. Deep down, we all know that we would have chosen this, even with all the pain that we have had to endure. I know the evil that Belle is going to send after us. I took her toy away, and now she will want to take something away from me. After all this I have learned that she doesn't let anything go, and she makes everyone pay, if they hurt her. I know we are strong enough for this, but I have and always will fear that one of us will not make it. We know we can be killed. That is how we lost Kara.

Crysta looks to find the vamp hunters. She and Leham go after them to bring them back to us. We need to stock up on our blood so the Boys go hunting and bring back seven vamps to fill the cages. Jacob and I stay at the lab, and I help as much as I can with the process.

"I didn't think we would be back so soon." Jason is smiling and laughing. He likes being with us, and couldn't wait to get back.

"Ok Rick you take over for me. I feel as if I have been nothing but in the way here." I turn and start for the tunnel.

"Thank you for letting us in on this Mikatta. It has been a long time since our family has gotten a real good fight with these lesser vamps. Yea, Crysta filled us in on everything that has been going on here while we were gone."

"No, thank you all for putting your lives in danger to help us, I know that you all can handle yourselves. To me, you are stepping into harms way. I do not wish for any of us to be hurt during this. I know with what she is sending at us, we will lose one or more of our family!" I finish walking down the tunnel so they cannot see the tears that fill my eyes.

Chapter Twenty Two
Preparations

With everyone gathered together we know what we must do. Now is the time for us to prepare for the battle that is to come. We do not want to have this battle on our turf. So we look for a place where we can have this fight. It needed to be far away from our home and the lab. We were all spending our time getting ready, stocking up on our food and food for the hunters as well. Every chance we get we practice our gifts. We needed to stay sharp. We were all on edge.

"Ok I think we have everything that we will need. Now we just need to find the battle ground." I have called a family meeting to see if anyone has found a place that we can take the fight to.

"Andrew and I found this old run down Ranch about three days run from here. Of course, we will have to carry the humans to get there in that time." Grady punches Jason in the arm. The two of them have found some sick fun in teasing each other.

"Oh, gee thank you almighty Dhampir. We would hate to slow you down!" He gives Grady a sad punch to the arm, but Grady pretends to flinch.

"Good, then we should get started. Every one carries something, or someone!" We all laugh. It isn't your full on, we are having the time of our lives laugh, but it is enough to relax us.

At the battle ground, as we call it, we had settled in rather well. There was no electricity or running water, but with the group we had that only lasted for a day. Kyle and Kelana were full-grown adults, just like Anthony. Unfortunately, I think that we still are not prepared enough for what is coming.

"MOM! They are coming." Crysta screams to me from the next room.

My link is instant I can link with everyone but the vampyer hunters. We have paired them up with one of us, that way they have a lesser chance of being hurt. Everyone is in place, so now we wait for the vamps to come to us. I can feel all the evil that is headed right to us. I try and feed off of the good energy that is all around us. Anthony is by my side, and we are ready to give aid to anyone of our family that is having any problems in their fight. They are coming at us from all around. They believe that they have us trapped. They forget, or should I say they don't know that we have God on our side, and we are never trapped! As they get closer Dawn calls to the wind and to the earth, she calls the wind to bring strong gust to knock as many of them to the ground as she calls to the earth to open up and let them in. Kelana pulls to her all the electricity that is in the air and all around us. With Anthony's and my help she sends out our second wave and fries as many of the lessers as she can. It is my turn now! I have built up as much energy as I can and Anthony and I walk out into the middle of the battle ground. We wait until they have gotten much closer to us. Then I force everything I have out and Anthony pushes it, with Leeha's help, out in a giant circle. For a moment, all you see is dust. Then as it clears you see that we have only taken out about half of them. The hand to hand fighting takes much more time. We are taking them out and so far no one has been hurt. Grady and Jason seem to be having way to much fun together. Andrew and Rick have kept up with them. I do believe that they were keeping count as to which team had the most kills.

It seems that we have almost taken them all out. Then I feel him, Samuel is at my back, I turn just in time to move out of the way of his fist. Grady and Andrew sense me and move right beside me. Before I know it the whole family has made a circle around me. What is left of the vamps and Samuel surround us.

"Well played Mikatta. I must say you seem to have a very strong family here. I smell humans among you. I think you have given yourself a weak spot my dear."

"We have no weak spots Samuel, but that is not what you have come for now is it. You have come for me! Belle wants me dead now that I have taken Kevin, or should I say Jason, away from her."

"Yes that has made her very upset. And this is what we have come to do. I can see now that I will not be killing you as she would like me to do. But, I will not leave here without taking some of you with me or should I say . . . killing some of you." Samuel uses the earth to force Jordan right into his hands Leeha tries to pull him out of Samuels's hands, but she doesn't have the strength. At this moment, everything seems to slow down for me. Everyone lashes out all at once trying to get to Jordan before Samuel can kill him. Jake gets right there and puts a stake into Samuels heart, but just as fast as that happened, Samuel pulled the stake out and sent it right through Jake's heart. Everyone is all over the place, and before anyone can stop him Samuel punches right through Jordan's heart. Everyone but I just stop. I can't stop myself. I feel as if I am flying, and before he even realizes what is happening my teeth are in Samuel's neck. Dan quickly moves to the other side of him and sinks in as well. We drain him faster than any of the other two. Then turn to try and help Jordan.

Once again, I bleed to try and save one of my children. Again, there is nothing that we can do. Jordan is gone! Leeha and Kyle both are kneeling by Jordan and there just are no words to describe the pain and sorrow that we were all feeling. It is at that moment that I remember that Jake too had been killed. I turn and Jason, Rick and Matt are praying over their lost friend. I go to them knowing there is nothing that I can do for Jake. As I almost get to them, I feel my head spin, and then I am floating. Or at least I feel as if I am floating. I look down and there I am lying on the ground, and I can see our whole family. Then I am right next to Jake and to Jordan.

"Am I dead as well?" I ask them because I have no idea, what is going on at this moment.

"No, Mom you are not dead. You were linked to me when I died. Remember we told you that your link had gotten stronger. So now you are here with me, don't worry you won't be staying. I need you to give something to Kyle for me." Jordan takes my hand and I feel energy pass between the two of us.

"It is part of your gift, how do I give this to him?"

"Just the same way I have given it to you. Tell Leeha I am sorry, and that there was never any other woman that I loved as much as I loved her. And tell Kyle that he needs to take care of his mother now that I cannot. Thank you Mom! Your love for me was something that I never really got from my own mother." Jordan kisses my check and then Jake is talking to me.

"Mikatta, can you tell my crew that I did what I did because I was told to. Not because I was trying to be some kind of hero or anything. And tell them to let my family know that I love them, and I will try and watch over them from this day forward? You're a wonderful leader Mikatta God has truly put his blessings on you." They both were gone, and I was back in my body.

The Ranch has been a very sad place for the past few days. The vampyer hunters have gone back to their families. They took Jake back to his family so they can bury him with the other hunters who have died during battles. Jason has told us that he will be returning as soon as the funeral is over with. Leeha has been in her room and just can't be comforted by any of the family. I know that I am the only one that can even come close to being able to help her through this. I knock on her door.

"Leeha dear may I come in and talk to you?" I ask, the question, even though I am going to go in no matter what she says.

"Yes Mom, you can come in." I am glad I don't have to enter without her wanting me there. I enter, and I sit next to her on the bed.

"Come my daughter, I have something I need to talk to you about." I pull her into my arms so I can pass some of my warming energy into her as I speak. "There is no one here, other than Grady that can truly understand what it is that you are going through. When I lost Kevin, I wanted to kill myself. That is the plain truth, and I felt as if no one could help me. Then Grady and Crysta came home to live with me. They could tell that I was not far from taking that step to join their Dad. The pain is very much unbearable, and nothing takes that pain away. It could take years before you even start to feel even a little better. I didn't think that I would ever be able to love again. Then there was Dan, and I see that everything happens for a reason. I love you daughter, so much that I have left you alone with your feelings, until now. You have a son, who doesn't understand what is going on. And he needs you right now more than ever." I look into Leeha's tear filled eyes and see that she has heard all that I have said.

"I understand Mom. I will go to Kyle. I know he needs me. Thank you for talking to me. I love you!"

"I have always loved you dear and always will!"

It has been a week since everything has happened, and I feel Jordan's gift wanting to be giving to his son. I have Leeha bring Kyle to me.

"Right after your Dad died do you remember that I fell to the ground as well?"

"Yes, I remember. Everyone thought that your connection to him might have killed you as well." Kyle is staying strong as he talks to me.

"Well, I was still connected to him, and I stayed with him for a little bit before he passed over. He wanted me to give you something Kyle. Would you like to have it?"

"Yes of course I would love to have something of my Dads."

"I will need to hold your hands grandson." I take Kyle's hands into mine and within seconds, I feel the energy pass between us. Kyle can't hold back the tears, and he begins to shake. I let go of his hands and hold him in my arms. My heart hurts for the loss of my son and I don't know how to make all of this better for my family.

"Leeha, here take your son. I think you two need some time together." Leeha understands that I need to get out of there I can't be strong any longer.

I run, for how long I can't remember, to get away from all the hurt and all the pain. I slow down and find myself in the middle of the woods. I must have run at least fifty miles from the Ranch. I stop and just sit down.

"Ok God, I need some help here! I don't know how we are going to be able to go on without Jordan. I know that we moved on after Kara's death, but Jordan was a husband and a dad. I don't think that I can fix all this. You said that everything happens for a reason, and I understand that. You are going to have to give me a little help here, because if any of the vamps attack us now, I think we might lose more of our family." I didn't think I would get an answer from him. I just needed to let him know that I was feeling really weak at this moment. Out of nowhere, I sense humans these are not the humans that we have been around. I try to hide behind a tree as they get closer to me.

"Mikatta, we know you're here somewhere. We were told to come here, to help you understand." It was a woman's voice, and there were three other humans with her. I walk out from behind the tree. "There you are, we are sorry we didn't mean to scare you, not that we could." She laughs to show that I do not scare her either.

"How did you know that I would be out here? Who sent you here?" I had made the decision to run. I didn't know I would end up here. So how could these humans know I would be here? The woman who was doing the talking was a tall woman with brown-hair and green-eyes. The other three look as if they were triplets, about my height and all with long blonde-hair and blue-eyes.

"Well, you should know who sent us. You were just speaking to him. We are here to answer your questions. You are very special Mikatta, and so is your family. They will be able to overcome this loss, just as the vampyer hunters have. Jason, Rick and Matt will be joining you very soon. They will help you and the others to get over the loss of Jordan. We are also here to tell you that your fight is far from over. But you now have a new gift that you have not realized yet."

"I don't feel any different. When would I have even received this gift? I haven't spoken with him since before the battle." I don't feel as if I have a new gift.

"Well then would you try doing something for me? Try and call the wind to you."

"You're joking right? I don't have that power that is Dawn's gift." There is no way that I could have that gift.

"Please just try to do this Mikatta." Reluctantly, I try to call the wind to me, when I did so the wind came to me and swirled around me. Then I tried to call the earth. I could feel it rumble under my feet. At that moment, all of my emotions came to the surface, and I begin to cry. Suddenly, the clouds roll in, and it starts to rain. Not a hard down pour, but a slow and soft rain. I look to see if the humans were still there, but they were gone. I fall to my knees as the rain falls down on me.

I return to a very upset family. I left and I have been gone for at least three hours.

"Do you know the worry that you have brought to this family! Crysta has been looking for you for hours. Why would you do that to us at this time? What is wrong with you?" Dan is yelling at me with so much fury. I can feel the pain in my heart, as if he is punching me right in the chest. I have used my new gifts, and they are still close to mind and with all the pain, he is creating, I just lose control and knock him to the ground with a huge gust of wind. Everyone just stares at me with a look of confusion.

"Mom, you can control the wind? How is that possible?" Leeha is not as upset with me as the rest of the family, because she knew why I had to leave.

"STOP EVERYONE JUST STOP!" Their minds are flooding me with their thoughts, and I can't take it. The earth rumbles and everyone's thoughts just stop. "Look I have just had the weirdest experience of my life, and as of late I have had quite a few of them." I tell my family what has happened to me and no one speaks. Dan has not even moved from the spot that I have thrown him into. I can't say I am sorry to any of them. I don't feel I should have to. With everything that I have been through and everything that I have had to do . . . No. I don't have to apologize!

"No Mom you do not have to tell any of us that you are sorry. You are the only reason that any of us are still here. It is us that owe you an apology." Out of nowhere Carrie speaks. "You have done everything for us, in fact everything you do is for us. So if you need to have some time to yourself, I think that we all should understand."

"I didn't mean, not to tell you where I was, but I truly had no idea what I was doing. I just needed to get out of the house. So I started to run, you know how fast we can run, I just couldn't stop. And before I knew it I was so far away. Next time I will be sure to let someone know of where I am." Still I do not feel I should apologize.

Chapter Twenty Three
Repairing the Damage

Dan and I have not spoken in days. I don't know what to do about what we have said and done to each other. Everyone else has come to me and apologized for getting upset with me, in fact, they have all tried to make me feel like I am the most wonderful thing in the world. I know that it is their way of trying to make me feel better. Still, Dan has stayed away from me. I haven't tried to speak with him either. Kelana and Anthony come to my room and sit on my bed.

"Ok I think that it is time for you and Dad to talk to each other. We are a family, and I feel as if we are falling apart. We need to be the way we were before. What if we get attacked right now? We don't have that connection that we need to fight back." Kelana is so wise and I know that she is right, but I don't feel I should be the one to start the damage repair.

"I know, but I don't feel I should have to be the one to do this. He came at me. I don't know how to fix this." Both of my children understand, and they hug me and leave. I truly don't know if we can fix the damage that Dan and I have done to each other.

"Hey dude!" Jason finds Dan out walking around the ranch.

"Hello Jason." Dan doesn't feel like talking to anyone right now.

"So You REALLY messed things up with Mikatta man!"

"Why do you say that I messed it up? She threw me against the wall. How am I the one that messed up?" Dan truly doesn't believe that he has done anything wrong.

"Wow man, you don't remember attacking her as soon as she got back? Would you like me to repeat the things that you said to her? I remember it all very clearly!"

"I guess I don't really remember what I said. I know that I told her that she should have told us she was ok." Dan still doesn't remember his verbal attack on me.

"Do you know the worry that you have brought to this family! Crysta has been looking for you for hours. Why would you do that to us at this time? What is wrong with you? Those are the words that you said to her before she had even had a little chance to tell you what had happened. And you were yelling, I believe at the top of your lungs dude!" Jason knows that he is treading on thin ice talking this way to Dan, but he also knows that Dan needs to be the one to apologize.

"I really said those things to her?" Dan is hearing the things that he has said to me and is starting to remember the day. "Oh God I swore to her that I would never do that to her again!" Dan hangs his head knowing that he is really going to have to do some real work to fix this. "What am I going to do? How can I ever say I am sorry enough or even in the right way so that she will forgive me?"

"I think you are going to have to go big or go home dude! We might need the help of the whole family for this one man."

Jason pats Dan on the back. "Wow you really did screw it up." Now Jason is laughing as he walks back to the Ranch with Dan.

"Hey Mom, can you please come out here?" Leham calls me to come out to the back porch. I walk outside to see my entire family, even Dan, standing in front of a hot tub that has a beautiful gazebo built around with lavender oils and real lavender growing around it.

"Wow, guys this is amazing, but why?" At that moment Grady is right behind me picking me up and carrying me to Dan. He places me right in front of Dan, and then all of my family members are gone. I am standing in front of my husband, alone for the first time in about a week.

"I don't know where to begin Mikatta. I don't know if you will believe me when I say that I am so sorry for what I did to you. I promised you that I would never mistrust you ever again, and that I would never talk to you that way ever. I have done both. I didn't realize what I had done until Jason shoved the memory in my face. I can't even begin to tell you how I feel about myself. I would understand if you couldn't find it in your heart to forgive me." Dan kneels down in front of me with his head hung. I want nothing more than to forgive him my heart is trying to forgive him as I look down at him. I place my hands on Dan's head suddenly I feel the pain in my husband's heart. I kneel down in front of him and make him look at me.

"I can always forgive you my husband. My love for you is that strong and that true. I cannot understand why you keep questioning me? You not trusting me is something that goes very deep. I can't get the feeling that you will never trust me out of my head. You swore that you would never mistrust me again. And you did it first chance you got. Have I not proven to you that I would never do anything that would harm you or this family? Or even myself, for that matter, our family and you are all that I live for! I need for you to help me understand your mistrust of me." With tears in his eyes, my husband looks at me again.

"You have not done anything that would give me any reason to not trust you. I am an asshole! There is no reason for you to be with me Mikatta. You deserve so much more than me. I have caused you so much pain. And you have done nothing to hurt me. I do not deserve you!" Dan begins to stand up to leave, but I pull him back down to me.

"Do you know what it means to be soul mates? It means no matter what our souls will never be apart. You are really going to have to kiss my ass for a while!" I smile at him and wrap my arms around his neck. Dan is so shocked. He picks me up and takes me inside the gondola and closes the door. He puts my face in his hands, and then he slowly leans in and gives me that first-time kiss. I am happy to be back in my husband's arms. As he kisses me, he slowly undresses me, I return the favor. Then he picks me up again but this time he places me in the hot tub.

"Ok now this I can get used to." I smile and laugh as he climbs in and pulls me on his lap.

"I gave you my words once before about not mistrusting you, and that I would never speak to you in that disrespectful way. I broke that, so I want to promise you and God that I will never ever do that to you again. I promise God, that I will never mistrust or disrespect her ever again. You gave me this wonderful woman and I have never done anything to deserve her." Dan pulls me even closer. "My love, I would like to make love to you."

"Well it is about time!"

"Hey Mikatta I would like to talk to you about something." Jason comes to me with a very serious look on his face.

"Of course Jason you know you are always welcome to speak with me. Is this about Rick and Matt? Because Crysta says that they will be here tomorrow morning."

"No, this is just about me. I know that you were turned into Dhampirs by drinking that blood packet."

"Yes, all of us have drunk from it. It took different amounts to change each of us. Why do you ask?" I do not like what I know Jason is going to ask me next.

"I want to become a Dhampir!"

"Jason why would you want to do this to yourself?"

"Because I feel that I can do more good if I join you all the way. I really do believe that I am meant to be one of you. I have felt it from the moment that I first met you. Please, before you just say no, talk to the rest of your family about it. And if it is possible to ask God, I would ask if you would do that as well."

"Jason, you know that I feel as if you, Rick and Matt are part of our family just as you are, right?"

"There is something inside my heart that tells me that I am meant to be just like you. I understand what all that means. I know the danger that I am putting myself in. I am telling you that I am meant to be a Dhampir." Jason truly feels that he is meant to be like us. He doesn't have a bad thought in that bald head of his. All he wants is to be more of a help then a hindrance.

"I will speak to the rest of the family about this. Jason I want you to think about this. You can never go back if you go through this change. Your life will never be the same."

"I understand what I will have to give up. I am willing to make that sacrifice if it means I can be more of a help to you Mikatta. If you haven't already noticed, I feel a bound to you. Not like I am in love with you are anything like that. In fact, I was the one to get Dan off his ass to make it right with you. More like I feel as if I am to be your protector. I don't know why I have that feeling, but it has been there from the day we met." These words that he speaks hit a cord with me. I knew in my heart that he would do anything that I asked of him no matter what. Maybe he is supposed to be a Dhampir.

"I will speak to the rest of the family about this matter."

"Thank you Mikatta that is all I can ask of you."

"MOM YOU HAVE TO COME RIGHT NOW!" The scream is from my son Anthony. I am at his side in seconds. In front of me lies Carrie. She is very close to having her belly torn apart by the baby inside her.